things

hoped

for

I want to thank Kaoru Suzuki for his insights about violin audition repertoire; Charles Clements for his perspective on the classical audition process; George Clements for what his music has taught me about composition and jazz performance; my wife, Rebecca, for her support and unfailingly accurate appraisal of my work; the superb editorial and copy editing staff at Philomel Books; and my editor, Patti Gauch, the best writing teacher I've ever had.

things

hoped

for

Andrew Clements

SCHOLASTIC INC.

New York Toronto London Auckland Sydney
Mexico City New Delhi Hong Kong Buenos Aires

PATRICIA LEE GAUCH, EDITOR

No part of this publication may be reproduced, stored in a
retrieval system, or transmitted in any form or by any means,
electronic, mechanical, photocopying, recording, or otherwise,
without written permission of the publisher. For information
regarding permission, write to Philomel Books, a division of
Penguin Young Readers Group, a member of Penguin Group
(USA) Inc., 345 Hudson Street, New York, NY 10014.

ISBN-13: 978-0-545-02295-8
ISBN-10: 0-545-02295-9

12 11 10 9 8 7   8 9 10 11/0

Printed in the U.S.A.   40

First Scholastic printing, September 2007

Design by Semadar Megged.

for my sister, Frances Clements Fawcett

things

hoped

for

chapter 1

THURSDAY

They say a sudden shock makes your whole life pass before your eyes. I can only speak for myself. In my case, they are correct.

At this moment my mind is a DVD player, and all my days are there, scene after scene, cued up for easy viewing. Except the thumping in my chest makes the pictures crackle and hiss. I scan, and then focus. I see a steep ravine in West Virginia, and a young girl, me, running barefoot through a hickory grove, playing tag with my little sisters, not a care in the world. That was over ten years ago. I push Fast Forward, then Play, and there I am at age fourteen, three years ago, alone in my bedroom, sawing away on my violin, imagining myself in an orchestra on the stage of a grand concert hall. And outside my bedroom, scattered around the rest of the house, I can feel my parents and brothers and sisters being driven slowly insane by my constant practicing.

I punch Fast Forward again to today, then Slow Advance. Because if I can get a better look at what happened this afternoon, maybe things will make more sense. Maybe my heart will stop pounding. Maybe I'll be able to breathe.

And on the small screen in my mind I see myself scurrying along 109th Street. I see myself arrive home from my violin lesson. It's about three-thirty. I'm sure of that, because Manhattan School of Music is about thirteen blocks away, and my lesson ended a little after three. It's a cloudy day in February with the wind whipping across the Hudson and into the city, so I want to get in out of the cold. I can feel the cold. My heart is racing and I can't catch my breath and I'm sweating as I remember. But I can feel the cold.

And I start up the front stoop of my grandfather's brownstone. There are nine steps. One, two, three—but I stop. Because I can hear the yelling. All the way through the brick walls and the triple-pane windows, I can hear the yelling.

I know that voice. It's Grampa's younger brother, my great-uncle Hank. There's usually yelling when Uncle Hank comes over, which isn't often, thank goodness. Not until recently. He lives on Staten Island, which is almost as far away as Connecticut. Grampa says he owns a recycling business down there.

And within one memory I'm suddenly having another one, about the day I met my great-uncle Hank for the first time eighteen months ago. He said exactly five words to me: "You must be Gwen, right?"

Right. I am Gwen. I was named after Grampa's wife,

Gwendolyn Page, my dad's mom. She taught writing and literature at City College for thirty-four years, and to hear my dad tell it, she was the one bright light of Grampa's life. And when Grandmother died three years ago, everyone thought Grampa would leave New York City, maybe move down to live with us in West Virginia. But Lawrence Page was tougher than that, and he stayed put. Daddy says he owns some rental properties in Queens. And then two years ago Grampa invited me to come north and stay at his home in Manhattan so I could study music here—an offer that seemed to come out of the blue. But I think my dad must have told Grampa about me and my violin. And maybe Grampa wanted some company too. All I know is that the invitation arrived just in time to keep me and the rest of my family from going completely crazy.

That first day I met Uncle Hank, when he asked me if I was Gwen, I didn't answer him. I only nodded, and that seemed to set the tone of our relationship. Ever since, when we see each other, we nod. My dad told me that Hank was a great guy, but I thought he'd be warmer toward me, like a real uncle. In old photos of him and my dad and Grampa on fishing trips, Uncle Hank always has this big grin on his face, standing there between them with his arms across their shoulders. Must have been happier times.

But I'm still reviewing the yelling scene. And me standing there on the front steps of my grandfather's house. On Thursday, earlier today. In the cold.

I shiver, and I see myself turn around, go back to the sidewalk, duck to the left of the stoop, take three steps down, and put my key into the lock on the iron gate. I swing it in slowly so the hinges don't squeal, then close it softly behind me.

And then it's like I'm in a small jail cell below the steps. The iron gate is on my left, there's a stone wall to my right, and in front of me is the door into the ground floor of the house.

I unlock the door and push it open. I'm planning to slip inside, walk along the hallway back to the basement door, and then creep down underground to the place I use as a practice studio. I can go to that sound-proofed room and play my violin anytime I want to. During these past three months I have spent at least five hours a day in there, rehearsing for my college auditions. I need that quiet little room. The endless rehearsing is frustrating because the music is so difficult, but when I finally break through and get it right, then all those maddening hours melt away like a dream, and I'm wide awake, and it feels like Bach or Sibelius or Paganini is right there in the room with me.

So at three-thirty on Thursday afternoon, I want to warm up my fingers and get on with my work. My whole life has been building toward these tryouts, and I wish I could go down to my studio and practice.

But the look on my face shows that I can't stand being home when Uncle Hank invades. During the past month he's come at least twice a week, and he yells from the moment he arrives until the second he leaves. And he always yells about the same thing. He wants Grampa to sell the building, this house. It's a four-story brownstone, like the places you see when they show the outside of the house on *Cosby Show* reruns. Grampa and Uncle Hank are joint owners of the building, but in their father's will it says Grampa can live here and collect the rent money for as long as he wants to.

So Uncle Hank yells that Grampa *has* to sell the house. That it's unfair *not* to sell it. He yells that Grampa is a selfish, stubborn old man. That each of them—Lawrence and Hank—could walk away with a million dollars, maybe more.

Uncle Hank isn't exaggerating about the money. A building like this in New York City is worth plenty. So Uncle Hank yells and yells and yells.

But Grampa doesn't yell back. It's never an argument. Grampa just says no. Quietly. The louder Hank yells, the more quietly Grampa says no. He won't argue, and he won't raise his voice. I don't know if Grampa even *could* raise his voice. These days, just talking without coughing is hard enough for him.

If I went down to the basement, and if I closed all the doors behind me, and if I shut myself into my rehearsal room, I wouldn't be able to hear the yelling. But it would still be going on, and I would know that. I would still feel it. Like the cold.

I see myself make a decision. I set my violin case just inside the door. I drop my backpack, unzip the front pouch, and grab a book. Then I go out the door, relock it, out the iron gate, relock it, step up onto the sidewalk, and turn right toward Broadway. There's a café half a block away, a place where I can be by myself but still have people around. Hot cocoa and a good book and the smell of fresh coffee. Much nicer than yelling.

And there I am alone at the café, on Thursday. I'm reading a collection of poems by William Butler Yeats. Again. For the third time this month.

I don't know why I'm stuck on Yeats.

There are hundreds of books in Grampa's study. It used to be Grandmother's study too, and she's the one who arranged all the books by genre, and then by the author's last name. I only met this grandmother once, at Christmas when I was five. She wrote in some of the books, no words, just penciled check marks and sometimes an exclamation point. It's not much to go on, but I think I would have liked to know her better.

Reading is the perfect break from the caprices and the partitas and the sonatas and scales and arpeggios I'm preparing for my auditions. And a few months ago I decided it would be good to read my way through the novels. I started with A for Austen, and I read *Pride and Prejudice*, which was so good that I immediately read it again. Then came *Wuthering Heights* (*B* for Brontë), and I even got to *Lord Jim* (*C* for Conrad) and *Robinson Crusoe* (*D* for Defoe). But I am constantly telling my own story to myself, and these days, that's about all the narrative flow I can handle.

I think that's why I shifted to poetry. And why am I hooked on Yeats? It's the density that I love, even though I don't get half his symbols. What I do get is that he looks at the life around him, and then he goes inward, digging until he finds something true. And I like how he's always imagining the world coming to an end. And I love his sadness. And his loneliness.

Thank you, Miss Page, for that sparkling literary commentary. While your heart is whomping away.

Because I'm still viewing the afternoon scene, still trying to catch my breath. And I can see myself settled into a booth with my book and my cocoa and some lemon cake. And then I glance up because I hear a voice through the glass, out on the street: "Taxi!"

I know that voice. I see Uncle Hank climb into a cab, see it turn across traffic and head south on Broadway. The yeller is gone. It is Thursday afternoon, and it's safe to go home.

But I don't. I have decided I need this break. I read and I sip and I nibble, and almost two hours pass in the coffee shop while I sail to Byzantium, and then to the lake isle of Innisfree, and then I go riding with the banshees, with Niamh calling *Away, come away.* And the next time I look up from my book, I see it's getting dark, and I need to get home and cook supper for Grampa. Because that's one of the few things he lets me do for him.

And in my mind I see myself go up all nine front steps this time.

And my heart beats even faster now, because I already know what happens next. I unlock the heavy oak door with the frosted glass and let myself into the entry hall where the staircase leads up to the third and fourth floors. A tenant has sorted today's mail, and after I unlock the door that opens from the hallway into Grampa's parlor, I pick up our pile from the narrow table. There's a letter to me from my mother.

Inside there is only one light on, the brass lamp with the green glass shade that sits on Grampa's huge desk in the study.

I call, "Hi, Grampa. It's me."

His bedroom door is shut, and there's no answer.

I walk through the parlor and into the study and put the mail on his desk. And I see the blinking light on the answering machine. So I push the button.

And Grampa begins to speak. On Thursday. Today.

Hello? Gwennie? I hope you had a good day. There's no easy way to say this, so I'm just going to tell you, straight out. I need to go and stay somewhere else—for how long, I'm not sure. I know this is sudden, but I have to leave right now, today. And I have to ask you to do something for me. I want you to keep the house going for me while I'm away.

Then Grampa coughs. A deep cough. I can tell he's turned away from the phone, but it's still loud. It hurts to listen. I've heard that cough a lot over the past three weeks, but he won't let me mother him. I have to pretend I don't see how he struggles.

Grampa begins again. His voice sounds weaker, and there are pauses when he has to catch his breath.

This is a lot to ask, Gwennie. I know that. But it's the best I can do on short notice. I need to go, right now, and I know you need to stay here. It's a hard situation, but we've both got to make the best of it.

Now, this is important. Please don't tell anybody I've gone. Especially Hank. I haven't changed my residence, but if he thinks I have, then he'll try to make something of it. Just steer clear of him. And please, don't judge him too harshly. Hank's having a tough time right now. Even so, I don't want him taking it out on you. And I don't think we should let anybody know that a high school girl is living here all on her own. I know you'll be fine, and you know it too. But others might not see it that way. So it'll be best not to tell anybody for now. I know this is a lot to bite off, but if I didn't think you could do this for me, I wouldn't be asking. And I am asking. And I thank you.

Grampa coughs again, and again it's hard for me to listen. Then he goes on.

You know where I keep my ATM card, and you know the PIN number. There's money in the savings account if you need to transfer more. And I signed some checks, in the black folder, second drawer of my desk. Gas and electric, bills like that get paid straight from the bank. Can't say what you'd need checks for—hard to know. But you treat that money like it's yours and . . . and you get whatever you need. There ought to be enough to last you through this stretch.

Well, I've got to get going. This business with Hank is tricky, so I'm not going to tell you where I'm staying, not just now. And I might be out of touch awhile. But don't you worry. And that's an order. You just keep about your own business and leave all the worrying to me. I love you, Gwennie. Good-bye now.

I listen to Grampa's message again, and then a third time, trying to understand. Trying to breathe slowly. Trying not to shiver.

And now, the actual now, I am sitting at Grampa's desk with one lamp burning. The streetlights are on outside, and a pale orange glow seeps through the tall front shutters.

In this city of ten million people, I am alone.

chapter 2

THE BRAVE ONE

After I listen to Grampa's message, my mind does not want to obey me, so I point it toward the green hills and the warmth of West Virginia. Thinking of home always calms me down.

And the first thing I picture is my two little sisters and my two big brothers. And my dad. And my mom.

Mama always says I am the brave one.

I can see her face on the day I tell her I want to go study music in New York. Mama could never imagine leaving her home. When she and Daddy got married, he moved south so she could stay put, close to where she was born and raised. And when I tell her I want to go and live with Grampa, she is mystified, but not surprised. I am the brave one.

For me, leaving West Virginia didn't feel brave. More like necessary. But it wasn't like I left all at once. I left molecule by molecule over a period of four or five years. Because when I started junior high school, I liked Nickel Creek and the Charlie Daniels Band and the fiddle playing of Alison Krauss as much as the next kid. But then I discovered Bach and Mozart and the rest of the gang, and classical music began pulling me away from the mountains, away from the deep woods and the rushing streams, and finally away from my family and friends in West Virginia. I started out liking the fiddle, but I fell in love with the violin.

And I can thank Mr. Richards for that, the music teacher at my junior high. He let me borrow some of his CDs, artists like Itzhak Perlman and Joshua Bell, and then Midori. And after four or five lessons with him, he convinced my folks I had some real talent. And then Mr. Richards helped me find a violin teacher in Charleston, and I was well and truly on my way. Away from West Virginia.

So by the time Grampa offered me free room and board in New York, the change was almost complete. I had to follow my new music. Mama understood, and so did Daddy. They didn't want to see me go, but they understood.

Still, it wasn't bravery that pushed me north. It was more like a survival instinct. The move was inescapable, but the journey wasn't without fear.

Even though it happened almost two years ago, the feelings are still with me. On that early August morning when I take my seat in the bus and turn to wave goodbye to my family, I think, This must be the hard part. Then five hours later the bus goes across the state line up into Pennsylvania, and I think, No, this is the hard part.

I sleep and I wake just as the bus dives like a whale into the Lincoln Tunnel, and then it plunges up and out into the gray air of the city. The harpooned bus spins around and around and comes to a gasping stop on the floor of the Port Authority terminal. I climb out, Jonah with a suitcase and a cheap violin, and I glide down four escalators to the street, and I climb into a yellow taxi, and I zoom sixty blocks north through New York City— and I think, This has to be the hard part.

And then a week later I go to my first day of classes at Latham Academy of the Performing Arts, and all the kids look at me and smile at my Charleston accent, and then I have to stand up and play a solo for our orchestra conductor, and I think, No, this must be the hard part.

And it was hard, because I hate soloing. The only good thing is that once the other kids heard me play, no one cared how I talked anymore.

All that is past, a year ago last September.

And here I am still sitting at Grampa's desk. On Thursday. Today.

I guess my mom is right. I don't frighten easily. But as the answering machine whines and rewinds, at this moment I do hope and pray that I have finally come to the hard part. And, of course, I'm pretty sure I haven't.

Grampa and I don't talk much, but over the past year and a half we've gotten used to each other. He has his routines, and I have mine. I know he likes having me around. He doesn't say that out loud, but he's been so kind, mostly little things, but some big ones too.

Like the practice room. That was huge. I'd been here two weeks, and one morning he says, "There's a carpenter coming over to fix up a room in the basement for you." Grampa said he didn't want to have to hear me playing all the time. And there was probably some truth to that. But it was more. It was a gift. He didn't want me staying late at Latham, or wasting time walking back and forth to the practice rooms at Manhattan School of Music. He wanted me to have a safe, quiet place to work. And he made sure the carpenter got everything just right. A gift.

I have always felt Grampa's presence in the next room, or down the hallway, or up a flight of stairs. We both like being alone, but we enjoy being alone together, the way toddlers like to sit side by side while they play in their own worlds. Sometimes I sit next to him and we watch *Wheel of Fortune*. Once he asked me to read a chapter of *Lord Jim* out loud. And two or three nights a week we have our bedtime snacks together. Simple moments. And already I miss that.

Sitting here in his worn leather desk chair on this Thursday night, I'm trying to understand what Grampa has asked me to do. He wants me to pretend he's still here. When we go on vacation, my dad hooks up timers to the lights. They turn on and then off, and the house looks lived-in.

And Grampa wants me to do that same thing here, now. Because of Uncle Hank and this valuable building? That makes sense. I think I understand that part.

And it occurs to me that my grandfather might be asking me to break the law. Because the law has a different word for pretending: fraud. And I have been to church enough to know what fraud is called in the Bible: bearing false witness. Lawrence Page, my grandfather, is asking me to lie for him.

If it were anyone else, I wouldn't even consider it.

I can hear the gold wind-up clock ticking on the mantel. It feels too quiet for this time of night, so I walk into the parlor and turn on Grampa's TV.

CNN. That's his channel. The news is bad, but the sound of it is good. If any of the people who live upstairs walk past the hallway door, it will sound like Lawrence the landlord is sitting in his easy chair, just like always.

And so I tell my first lie. For Grampa.

My cocoa and lemon cake have worn off. I go to the kitchen and fix myself a cheese omelette and then sit at the small dining table and eat. Omelette, toast, orange juice, milk, alone.

Alone is not a problem for me. I couldn't count the hours I have spent alone. Alone in the woods. Alone in my room. Alone in the library. Alone in a book. Alone in my music. I'm comfortable alone.

Because being a classical musician isn't like sitting on the front porch playing the fiddle with a bunch of friends. It's more like a long hike on a lonely road. It's ninety-five percent solitary practice time, two percent instruction time, two percent rehearsal time, and one percent performance. Nothing is improvised, and if you're not a perfectionist, and if you don't like being on your own a lot, then you need to go and find yourself another road.

And with such an intense schedule, there aren't a lot of opportunities for making friends. Or for meeting boys. There's just no time for that. At least not so far. Not for me. But maybe I'm only making excuses for not trying harder.

Because I notice guys, and I've been known to smile at one now and then. I mean, I don't want to be on my own forever. Or living with my grampa for the rest of my life—not that there's any risk of that.

But that thought brings back my worries, and I have to push away the fears about Grampa.

And then I try to remember what I ought to do next, right now, tonight.

With Grampa having trouble, it feels selfish to think about me, but I can't help it. I can't ignore what's going to happen in five days. I am crashing toward the end of my senior year in high school, and this coming Tuesday I have an audition at the Juilliard School, and then the next afternoon an audition at Manhattan School of Music, and then two days later I have to be at the New England Conservatory in Boston. There are other auditions in mid-March, but Juilliard, Manhattan, New England—those are my big three, and they are soon.

The faculty members at these auditions won't want to hear me gush about how I've loved music since I was a little girl in the hills of West Virginia. They won't want me to tell them how I felt the first time I listened to Beethoven's Sixth Symphony, or how I wake up with melodies running through my head, and how thrilling it is to let the sounds in my mind rush across my fingertips and spray into the air that surrounds my violin. They won't want me to talk at all. They only want to hear me play.

I have practiced my violin thousands and thousands of hours during the past ten years, and now my musical future depends on how well I play during those three auditions, twenty minutes each.

And suddenly, this new complication. More pressure is not what I need.

But it's Thursday night, and I force myself to stay positive. I tell myself that with Grampa away, things might actually be easier. Because who's been doing all the shopping and a lot of the cooking for the past six months? And who gets herself up and off to school every day? And who sets her own schedule, and puts herself to bed each night? Does anyone wait up if I'm out late at the Philharmonic or when I go get food with my friends after rehearsals?

Grampa hasn't been taking care of me. More like the other way around, when he lets me. I have been mostly on my own in this city for a long time. And I've been worried about Grampa for a long time too. I'll come in late from a rehearsal, and he'll be under his fleece in that big recliner in front of the TV, looking so small and old. And I'll be afraid to shake him, afraid that he won't wake up.

A knock, and I jump from my chair.

A voice from the hall. "You there, Lawrence? It's me, Jason."

I can't move.

A second knock. "Lawrence?"

It's the tenant from the studio apartment at the back of the house on the fourth floor. I walk across the parlor, turn the deadbolt, and open the door six inches.

"Hi, Jason. Grampa's in the bathroom. Can I give him a message?"

Lying shouldn't feel this easy.

Jason's about thirty. Short dark hair, brown eyes, stocky build, white T-shirt and jeans. He's been eating garlic.

"Yeah, sure, Gwennie. Just tell him that the ceiling leak I told him about earlier? It stopped. Maybe iced up or something. But it'll be back. So he needs to get a roofer over here. That's all. And tell him I mailed that envelope for him." A pause, a big smile, then, "So, how's the music business? Your grampa's so proud—tells me about you all the time. He says you've got auditions coming up, right?"

I smile back. "Next week."

"Good luck, okay?"

"Thanks."

Jason turns and heads for the stairs, and I shut and lock the door. And I'm a little surprised. Because Grampa doesn't seem like he's that proud of me. Or even paying much attention. Of course, it could be me. Maybe I'm the one who's not noticing things.

A leak. That means a repairman. And I have to be here to let him in so he can get up to the roof through the metal lid at the end of the fourth-floor hall. And I have to check over the work he does. And I have to pay him. All without Grampa. And without letting on that Grampa isn't here.

But it's Thursday evening, and I force myself to stop thinking about this, about any of it.

I walk downstairs. I go to the ground floor door, turning on lights as I go. I pick up my violin case. The roof has a leak, and I need to deal with that. And Grampa's gone, and I need to deal with that. But more than anything else, I need to practice the Paganini Caprice in B Minor, number 2. And then caprice number 17 too, and then all the rest of my pieces. I don't just need to get into a good school. No, I need to audition so well that people will want to give me a scholarship, pay me to come to their school. Free room and board here with Grampa has been a godsend, but I know it's temporary, same as my scholarship at Latham. If I want to keep going forward, I need to make my own way.

I walk down more stairs to the basement, open the door to my rehearsal room, flip the light switch, and shut myself in.

I unzip the case and take out my violin. It's not actually mine. My own violin is in my bedroom closet. I've been told it would make good kindling. This violin in my hands is on loan from the school, "provided to a promising student"—which means loaned to a kid whose parents can't spend twenty or thirty thousand dollars for a good instrument.

With the right care, a violin will live forever. And if a violin gets dropped or comes unglued, a specialist will resurrect it. This one was made in Italy in 1883. Dozens of other musicians have used this violin, and a lot of them are dead and gone. Someone else will be playing this violin long after I have died. It doesn't matter that I don't own it, because I'm just the player of the moment. I borrow everything. Violin, music, air, water, time, this practice room—everything's on loan. And I have to prove that I deserve it.

I lay the violin on the stool and get out the bow, also very expensive, and also borrowed. I tighten the nut and rub the horsehair across the rosin a few times. Then I lay my mother's white silk handkerchief on the chin rest, raise the violin to my shoulder, take a deep breath, and begin.

When I have to play a solo piece like this caprice, sometimes it helps if I imagine a scene. Because I don't like standing up in front of people and playing alone. I've never wanted to be a soloist. I guess it's the same shyness I've had since kindergarten. That's why I love the orchestra. I want to be nestled there among the first violins, rows and rows of us, and there's me, almost invisible in my black concert dress. I want to play my part perfectly, but I don't want to be seen.

So as I play caprice number 2, I imagine that I'm a serving maid, and I have to carry a silver tray loaded with fine china from the kitchen all the way up a marble staircase to the sitting room of a fussy old woman. Up and up the stairs I hurry on tiny feet, but careful, because one false step will send me and the tray crashing down the steps. And then there's a call from below—someone forgot the marmalade. And I turn quickly and balance the clinking china all the way back down. And then halfway up a second time, a damask napkin flutters off the tray, and I have to turn around again.

Up and down, up and down I go, each note a footstep, until finally, every obstacle is overcome, and with a flourish I sweep through the doorway of my lady's room—and luncheon is served.

This caprice is killing me. More precisely, I am killing this caprice. And that's sad. I know it's such beautiful music, fluid and elegant, and I know I'm not doing it justice. Which is what my teacher demands. He's Russian, very dramatic. He'd make a good Jane Austen character.

At yesterday's lesson Pyotr Melyanovich said, "The composer begs you to keep him alive. When you play his *capriccio*, he stands behind you, listening. If your playing is weak, the composer weeps. He mourns for himself. If you cannot play his music, Paganini will die."

Praise from my teacher is like water in the Sahara. One rare day I played well, and he said, "You have the gift, little one—the heart and the soul." A sip of praise. It keeps me trudging forward on this Thursday night, with thousands of notes lit up in my mind, tiny stars in a desert sky.

This caprice is less than three minutes long. My practice rule is simple: Play the whole piece from beginning to end; at any mistake, start over. At the end of an hour I have played it through completely only twice.

My fingers and my bow have to dance with perfect grace across the same four strings. One false step and I've ruined the intonation, botched the rhythm, destroyed the dynamics, choked the flow. And for my auditions, I have to play every note from memory.

I have two more lessons before my first audition. And that's good. This West Virginia girl needs all the help she can get.

The second hour on the other caprice is better. Paganini is still on life support, but he's breathing. Perhaps tomorrow he'll be able to sit up and take some nourishment through a straw. Then I spend an hour on my Bach partita, and then I run through the first movement of the Sibelius concerto.

And then it's time for food and rest. I'm an athlete, and this is my training camp.

Walking up to the first floor, the house feels too still. I can still hear CNN, but I know it's only noise. And when I turn off the TV, the silence is complete. There's no traffic on 109th Street, and even if there were, the brick walls are eighteen inches thick, and all the windows are triple-glazed. The upstairs tenants are quiet. I wish I could hear Grampa snoring through his bedroom door.

"Is the perimeter secure?" That's what Grampa asks me every night. It's from his years in the army. And after I check all the doors and windows, I report back, "Perimeter secure, sir." And then he salutes me. Every night. Until now.

So after I've locked up, I toast some raisin bread and drink a glass of milk. When Grampa joins me for an evening snack, he likes his milk warmed up. And he has a cookie or two, never toast.

Cooking just for myself is going to be simpler. So I guess that's one good thing.

When I go into the study to turn off the desk lamp, I see the stack of mail from this afternoon. And I remember: I have a letter from home.

I carry it downstairs to my bedroom and lay it on my pillow. When I'm ready, I climb into bed, open the letter, lie down on my side, and begin to read.

February 8
Dear Gwendolyn,
It was good to talk to you last Sunday. I saw George Robbins, and he said he'd had an e-mail from you. I keep asking for a computer of my own, but your father says we don't need one at home since he's al-

ready got one at work. A lot of good that does when your sisters need to type their schoolwork. Half the time when you send us a message, your dad forgets to tell me, and then I have to remind him three times to print it and bring it home. And I have to say, an e-mail isn't near as nice as a real letter in the mailbox.

We're all fine here. Except James isn't liking his job at the garage. Boys shouldn't try to work for their dads, if you ask me—which nobody ever does. I have told James a dozen times that I would help him with college costs, and I think he might be starting to listen to me. And it's about time.

Harlan's steady as a rock. He's just started working for a big insurance company in Charlotte, and he says he likes it. He doesn't get home as often as I'd like, but you know me. If I had my way we'd just keep making this house bigger, and you could all live here with me forever.

Sharon's been to three dances with three different boys in the past month. I worry about that child, but I don't think she's anywhere near as boy crazy as I was, once upon a time. Carolyn seems a little more sensible, but she's still young yet—getting straight As too.

I've got the schedule you sent me on the wall in the kitchen where I can see it every day, and I pray that you are happy. I don't know how you can stand that city, except I know it's where your music is.

Your Uncle Belden asked me again if you won't send him a recording of your playing. I think he has told every man, woman, child, and dog in this part of the state that he's the one who gave you your first fiddle. He is so proud of that. You know he'd be happy with any little thing. Not right away, I know, because of your college tryouts. But it'd mean the world to him.

I'm going to bed now. You keep safe. He may not show it, but I know Grampa Page loves having you there as much as I hate having you gone. He's been awfully good to you, so you say thanks every chance you get.

I'm counting the days until June. You're always in my prayers.

With all my love,
Mother

I fold the letter and tuck it with the others in the drawer of my nightstand.

I feel bad about Uncle Belden. I had to make a CD of my playing to send along with my college applications—prescreening just to get an audition. These schools want to hear a recording first to see who deserves to try out in person. I could have burned an extra CD and sent it to Uncle Belden. And I should have, but I didn't.

People hear I'm from West Virginia and right away they think poverty and dirt floors and hog farms down in the holler. My folks are about twenty minutes outside Charleston, and where we live it's not like that. My dad has his own car repair business, and my mom finished two years at the junior college before she started her family. I guess we're middle-class Americans. Still, every radio button in both the car and the pickup plays country. And not just because that's all there is to choose from.

We don't have a lot of money, but we've never been poor. Now, my mom's family, they're poor. They live in the hills about two hours east. Not dirt-floor poor, but pretty close. They live scruffy, and it would be hard to say how much money my dad's loaned them over the years. Hard for me to say, I mean. I'm certain that Daddy knows to the penny.

Uncle Belden is my mom's brother, and it's fair to say he's the reason I'm here in New York, even more than Mr. Richards. When I was little and we'd visit, he'd always play his fiddle. He had the magic, and everybody listened, even Daddy. It's almost my earliest memory, sitting on my mom's lap, listening to that sound, and then wailing for more when it stopped. Belden knew. He told my mom, "That Gwennie, she's got the music, you wait and see."

Turns out we didn't have to wait long. I was four and Belden gave me a one-fourth-size violin for Christmas. He put the tiny fiddle in my hands and showed me how to tuck it under my chin, how to hold the bow up and scrape it back and forth across the strings. And to me it all felt as natural as jumping in the creek on a hot afternoon.

Every time we went up into the hills to visit, Belden and I would play for hours. We found the most amazing harmonies. And when I was ten, Belden declared, "This child knows more 'bout fiddlin' than I do!"

And thinking of that simple time makes my eyes smart. But I blink hard and turn off my lamp. And I make myself promise to send Uncle Belden a CD. And I make myself stop wondering how Grampa's doing, and how I'm going to get the roof fixed. And I make myself stop worrying about my auditions. And then I make myself close my eyes and say a prayer and rest. And I make Thursday come to an end.

Because I am the brave one.

chapter 3

TIGHTROPE

She is balanced on a tightrope, thin as an E string. There is only emptiness below, and the rope slants upward. In the mist above her there must be a place to rest, a platform she can cling to, but she can't see it. Wind and rain slap at her from behind. There is no going back, and there is no net. And as she tries to take her next step, the rope goes slack. She is dropping into the darkness. And as she falls, I sit up, bed drenched with sweat, breath rasping in my throat.

Then my alarm clock goes off.

First I remember that I'm Gwen. And then that I'm in New York. And then that it's Friday morning, with only four more days until my first audition. And then I remember Grampa's phone message. Four items.

I can only deal with the first three. Because the fourth one is too upsetting.

I think maybe I should get out the Yellow Pages and call every hospital in the city until I find him. Because

I don't want him to be alone. If he needs help, I'll help him. Did he think he couldn't ask me, that I'm that preoccupied, that selfish? And I'm almost angry at him for putting me in this situation, for making me feel so guilty. And helpless.

But I make myself be logical, and I remember that Grampa might be old and frail, but he's still his own person, and he can do whatever he wants. And I remember what he told me to do: *You just keep about your own business and leave all the worrying to me.* That's not going to be easy.

But really, I'm glad Grampa gave me that order, because on Friday I can't afford to spend a single minute sitting around wringing my hands. And I can't stay by the phone trying to make it seem like he's here at home either. So I make a decision.

In twenty minutes I'm on the subway headed south, and fifteen minutes later I'm on a bus headed for the East Side. Latham Academy of the Performing Arts is a private school, and all the classes are small, only five or six kids. I could never afford it if I hadn't gotten a full scholarship. It doesn't feel like high school—more like tutoring sessions, and the academic classes meet only four days a week from nine to noon.

Because, really, Latham is a conservatory, a music school. Music theory, solfège, harmony and counterpoint, music history, sight reading—it's excellent and it's demanding. No way would I have been accepted into the Tanglewood Institute last summer if I hadn't had this kind of teaching.

Tanglewood was heavenly. Lessons and master classes in the morning, practice time all afternoon, then rehearsals, performances now and then, and in the evenings and on weekends, the Boston Symphony. And the Berkshires were almost as pretty as the mountains back home.

But even in that perfect setting, there was tension, this undercurrent of competition, with all the violinists checking each other out. Because I know the kids I studied with there in Massachusetts last summer are the people I'll see again and again at auditions and competitions and festivals for the rest of my musical career. If I ever have a musical career.

At nine-thirty Mr. Ware is leading a discussion of *The Sun Also Rises*, but I am replaying last night's practice session in my mind, deciding which parts of each piece need the most work. And the part of my mind that isn't thinking about my auditions is worrying about Grampa.

At ten-thirty my physics teacher is explaining surface tension and capillarity, but all I can hear is the cadence of the sarabande in my Bach partita. And Grampa's message, replaying in my head for the tenth time.

By noon on Friday I am dying to get to a practice room, but I make myself eat lunch first. I know I'm going to need the fuel. When I tried to skip dinner one day, Grampa told me, "Every officer knows that an army marches on its stomach. So does an orchestra, and don't you forget it. Now sit here and eat a real meal. And that's an order."

Marcy sits down across from me in the lunchroom. She plays cello, and we're in a chamber group together. I have sat beside this girl for dozens of hours, and we've played Mozart and Haydn and Bach together, gorgeous music. Her notes and my notes weave in and out and all around each other, but they never actually touch. She makes sounds, and I make sounds, and the vibrations meet in the air, and when the sounds are right, both of us smile. But does that make us friends? I don't think so. And that's probably my fault. To really be her friend I'd have to give up some of my time. All I've been willing to share so far is my music stand.

"So, are you ready for your Juilliard audition?"

Marcy's all bright and bubbly. She can afford to be. She's a junior.

I try to smile back. "Not completely. But I know what I have to do."

She nods and says, "Oh, I know what you mean."

But she doesn't know. She's just a junior, and audition madness is still a year away for her. She has no idea.

I'd like to chat, to be friendly and polite. I want to, but I can't, not right now. And I'm glad Marcy doesn't seem to mind.

"Mark, he's got an audition at Curtis next week. He plays viola, remember? And he is such a *mess* right now—as if a bad audition would be the end of the *world* or something."

Marcy doesn't get it yet. She's talented, but she doesn't get it.

Because her boyfriend's right: A bad college audition *is* the end of the world. Or at least it's the end of one world. It means you have to go and find another world to live in—a world that's not about studying with a great teacher, or learning new pieces, or mastering an instrument, or playing music for a living. A world that's less perfect. A world where music might become a sad, wistful hobby.

I'm done with my sandwich and I finish my milk and I smile at Marcy. "See you later."

"Okay, and good luck on your auditions, Gwennie."

"Thanks."

I walk up the winding staircase to the third floor and go to my favorite practice room.

Good luck. Everybody says "good luck."

I open the case and rosin my bow.

It's not about luck. Mr. Ware has a quote by Ralph Waldo Emerson on the wall in my English classroom:

Shallow men believe in luck.
Strong men believe in cause and effect.

I close the practice room door and begin my warm-ups. Fingers, strings, pressure, bow, friction, sound. Cause and effect.

Emerson gets it.

An hour into the practice my cell phone rings. I don't

know the number, and I almost reject the call. Then I remember: This could be Grampa.

I catch the call on the fifth ring. "Hello?"

"Is this Gwen?" It's a man's voice.

"Who is this?"

"Lawrence Page gave me your number. I'm Kenneth Grant, his attorney."

"Oh—Grampa called you?" Because that would be wonderful news.

"No, I got a voice mail from him late Thursday afternoon, very brief. But in the message he asked me to check up on you. I don't really know why he wanted me to call. So . . . everything's okay?"

"Yes—fine." Grampa's paying this lawyer three hundred dollars an hour to see if I'm all right. It's ridiculous, but it makes me feel good anyway.

"And you're a music student, right?"

"He told you that?"

"Yes. And you're in college?"

"Not yet."

The lawyer pauses. "So, what's going on with Lawrence? Is he okay?"

That tells me Grampa hasn't told this man about him leaving.

More cautious, I say, "Sure—fine. He's fine," but I don't believe that.

Neither does Kenneth Grant. Picking his words, he says, "You know, your grandfather's been my client for twelve years now, and I've known him all my life. And if he needed some help—or if you needed any help—it would be all right to tell me about that. I know how he's under pressure to sell his house. I know about his brother, his finances, his health, everything."

I can feel how nice it would be to talk with this man, to ask him for advice. But Grampa's instructions on the answering machine are clear: Please don't tell anybody.

So I say, "Grampa naps a lot, and I think he gets worried about me being out around the city all day. And sometimes I don't get home until after dark. He gets worried. That's all."

A long pause, and then Mr. Grant clears his throat. "So you don't think it's odd that I've tried to reach your grandfather six times since nine-thirty this morning and he hasn't answered, hasn't called me back? You think he's just napping a lot?"

I'm not ready to play this game, and it shows. "Um . . . he might have walked over to the park. Or maybe he's been with some friends at the coffee shop. Down the block."

"Oh. So he's doing better with stairs now?"

"Yes . . . much better."

This man knows I'm lying, but I don't care. I don't want to talk about Grampa, or think about Grampa or worry about Grampa. And I need to get back to Sibelius. So I say, "Well, thank you for calling me, Mr. Grant. I'm sure this will make my grandfather feel better."

"All right," he says. "My cell phone number's in

your phone now, so if you need anything, either of you, call me. And I mean that. You probably don't know this, but Lawrence saved my dad's life in Italy in 1943, took a bullet in the leg doing it. If it wasn't for your grandfather, I wouldn't be here. And I live close by, right at Riverside and Ninety-fifth, so you can call me day or night, okay?"

"Okay."

"Good-bye, Gwen."

"Good-bye."

It takes me ten minutes to bottle up a fresh batch of fears about Grampa, and ten minutes more to get back into the concerto. I play for another hour, but my heart's not in it now. I can't shake the feeling that things are skidding, sliding out of control. And I hate feeling so powerless.

At two o'clock I leave school and head for the crosstown bus that will drop me at Seventy-second and Broadway for the subway ride up to my lesson. Because that's something I *can* control. I can be on time. My lesson begins at three-fifteen on Fridays, and if I'm even a minute late, Pyotr Melyanovich locks his door. It only happened once. "Do you think you can rush out onto the stage after the concert has begun?" he shouted at me through the wall. I haven't been late since.

It's a sunny afternoon, and the bus sails across Central Park, and the subway gets me close to my neighborhood a little after two-thirty. I've got all kinds of time, so instead of riding directly up to 116th Street, I get off at 103rd. Because I'm going to stop in at home so I can dump my schoolbooks and grab a snack. And I'm also going to stretch my legs in the process and try to breathe in some real air, or as real as air ever gets around here.

· This city is great for walking, especially when the weather's right. And considering it's February, there's nothing to complain about. It's one of those false spring days, the kind that brings New Yorkers out of their caves for an afternoon stroll. All the produce shops on Broadway have flowers spilling out onto the sidewalk, buckets and buckets of them, and I can't resist buying a huge bundle of daffodils. And they make me think of that poem—

> I wandered lonely as a cloud
> That floats on high o'er vales and hills,
> When all at once I saw a crowd,
> A host of golden daffodils;

I found that in a Wordsworth collection. He's really good. He doesn't get to me like Yeats does, but he knows how to paint a scene so I can't forget it.

I get home, go in on the ground floor, drop everything but the flowers, and run upstairs. A minute later I'm in the kitchen with my mouth full of sliced turkey, and I'm pouring a glass of milk, and I glance across the parlor. And I can see into the study. Because the desk lamp is on. And I see a shoulder. Of someone sitting there. At Grampa's desk.

I choke on the turkey, and I croak, "Grampa?" Because it has to be Grampa. It has to be. But it's not. The man stands up, and Grampa's not that tall. And the man turns around. Then he smiles. An amused smile.

It's Uncle Hank.

"Probably surprised you." He sees how shaken I am, and he keeps smiling. "Where's Lawrence?"

"I . . . I just got home."

"You saw him this morning?"

I nod and reach for the paper towels to wipe up the milk I spilled. My heart is tapping out sixteenth notes.

"Not like him to be out on a Friday afternoon. I called and left a message I was coming." Another smile. "Maybe that's why he's not here. So I used my key."

I hate him being here. Grampa would hate it too.

It's two-fifty-two on Friday afternoon, and I have to leave, but I can't, not with the answering machine sitting right there on Grampa's desk. If Uncle Hank plays Grampa's message, he'll put me out of this house. So he can sell it and get the money. He'll make me leave, I know he will. I'll be shipped off home. Or maybe forced to move in with some friend from school. Not that I actually have a friend like that.

And truly, it wouldn't matter where I'd be sent, because this close to my auditions, the effect would be the same—disaster. Because I need my routine, and this quiet house, and my practice room. I'm on the tightrope, the one in my dream. I'm on it, and I'm alone, and I have to get across it. One little jiggle, and everything will change. Everything.

Because my whole life's story has been building up to these tryouts. I need to keep my balance, take my auditions, get my scholarships. I need to stay on the tightrope. Me and my borrowed violin. I need to get to that next platform. Because there's no net.

And as I stare at Uncle Hank, it's time to leave for my lesson. Because I have to be there on time. I *have* to.

I clench my jaw, and I say, "Grampa doesn't want you in here. In his home. He told me. So you should leave." My voice sounds strong, braver than I feel. Because I'm speaking for my grampa now. And I say it again. "You have to leave now."

"Oh, really?" Hank smiles again, still amused. "I *have* to? Is that what I heard? You're *telling* me that I have to leave?"

"Yes," I say. Then I hold up my cell phone. "And Grampa's lawyer. He'll tell you too. Shall I call him? His name is Kenneth Grant."

Uncle Hank's face changes when I say that name—less smile. I push on. "And I already talked with Mr. Grant once this afternoon. And he said if Grampa needs any help, or if I need some help, all I have to do is call him. And it's time for you to leave Grampa's house now. So, should I call Mr. Grant? Do I need some help? Do I?"

He looks at me. Grampa said not to judge him too harshly, but I'm losing that battle. I can't believe this person is Grampa's brother. His lips keep smiling, but not his eyes. He shrugs. "You don't need help. Not yet. But you might if your daddy knew you were sassing me like this." He crosses to the parlor door and opens it. "I was ready to leave anyway. When you see Lawrence, you tell him to call me. It's important. Good-bye, Gwennie," and he yanks the door shut so hard that a painting on the opposite wall shakes and tilts to a crazy slant.

I run to the door and chain it, my hands shaking. And then I slam the Fox lock in place, the long steel rod that leans between the door and a slot in the floor. Uncle Hank might have a key to the deadbolt, but Grampa added Fox braces to the three outside doors just a month ago. And there are only two keys, Grampa's and mine. And the brace-release locks have Medeco cylinders— pick-proof. New York turns everyone into a lock expert.

I scramble downstairs, trot past my bedroom, past the door to the basement, through the laundry room and into the utility room, and I put the brace rod in place against the door to the backyard.

My pulse is still racing, and as I go back through the utility room, the compressor on the big freezer kicks in and I nearly jump out of my shoes. I'm at the ground floor door and I only have thirteen minutes to get to my lesson. I use the straps and put my violin on my back. I put the brace rod into its groove, and when I close the door and turn the key in the cylinder, I hear it settle into place with a solid clunk that seems to echo through the whole empty house.

"Perimeter secure, sir."

I trot over to Broadway, and I flag a cab because I have to be on time for my Friday lesson. I *have* to be. Grampa would want me to be on time. Even if it meant that I had to leave my beautiful daffodils gasping in the kitchen sink.

And I am on time. I make it to the third floor studio with only a minute to spare. Because I *will* have my lesson today. I will play my best for Pyotr Melyanovich, and he will teach me to play even better.

I have earned this tightrope, and I *will* move ahead. I *will* get to the next level—no wishing, no dreaming, no luck.

Cause and effect.

chapter 4

FAMILIAR FACE

A good lesson is when my teacher doesn't scold me. A great lesson is when Pyotr Melyanovich smiles or nods.

Friday's lesson is better than great. When I play the runs and the double stops of caprice number 17, there is a smile. When I plunge into the third movement of the Sibelius concerto, after eight measures, there is a nod.

I've heard other kids at my school talk about their private teachers, and our experiences are all so similar. Any one of us would walk through fire if we thought that would make our teachers approve of our playing, or compliment the tiniest bit of progress. It's scary how much power Pyotr Melyanovich has over me, over my life and how I feel about myself as a musician. I want this strange little man to be so proud of me, proud to call me his student, proud that I've begun to master another difficult piece, proud that his teaching has helped me ace an audition.

A smile *and* a nod. A superb lesson.

On the way home I stop at the café on Broadway to give myself a small reward: cocoa, cake, and Yeats.

As I try to decide how large my cocoa should be, it occurs to me that it's nice not to have to rush home to see how Grampa's doing. And immediately I'm ashamed of myself for having such a selfish thought. But then I have to admit it's still true.

And while I'm having my little truth-telling session, I notice a guy behind me in line. Actually there are three guys: one wearing a greasy Mets cap, one in a suit and topcoat talking too loud on his cell phone, and one wearing khakis and hiking boots with a trumpet case hanging from his shoulder. He's the one I mean, the boy with the trumpet.

I'm in a booth a few minutes later and I've got my book open, and the trumpeter comes and stands there until I look up.

When I first got to town, I thought that there were West Virginia rules, and then there were New York City rules. But now I know that's not true. People are people. Still, I decide I should go with the old city rule that applies to a moment like this: Don't be too nice.

I give him the stony eye. "This table's taken."

He shakes his head, smiling. "Just a quick question." He points at my violin. "I thought you might be able to tell me how far I am from Manhattan School of Music."

I'm still made of marble. "It's about a fifteen-minute walk. North on Broadway to 122nd Street."

"Great. Thanks." He's got a nice smile. Straight brown hair. A good face. Doesn't talk like he's from New York. Of course, neither do I. Almost nobody here is actually *from* New York, not originally.

Before he turns away, I want to ask him what he's doing at Manhattan School. But I don't, and he's headed toward the door.

I go back to my Yeats anthology, where I'm into this batch of poems that he published in 1899. The ones about this woman he loves are my favorites, and I keep coming back to a poem called "He Wishes for the Cloths of Heaven." Grandmother put an exclamation point in the margin, and I've added one of my own.

Had I the heavens' embroidered cloths, . . .
I would spread the cloths under your feet:
But I, being poor, have only my dreams;
I have spread my dreams under your feet;
Tread softly because you tread on my dreams.

I look up and I blink my way back to the coffee shop, because the boy with the trumpet is standing there again, still smiling. "I know this table is taken, but could I just sit a second and finish my drink?"

I nod, and he moves my violin and sits across from me.

I try to read, but I can tell he keeps looking at me. I can feel my face beginning to turn pink.

Then he says, "You were at Tanglewood last summer, right?"

I nod. "Yes."

"I *knew* I'd seen you before. I've got a good memory for faces. And other things. I've just got a plain old good memory."

I say, "Were you there for the orchestra session?"

"Yeah, and the brass workshop too. It was a great summer."

I nod. "For me too. Sorry I didn't recognize you. The violin program was really intense. I didn't socialize much." Which must make me sound like a total music geek. Which is pretty much true.

My face still feels warm. I ask, "What are you doing at Manhattan School?"

"Today? Nothing, just looking around. And maybe I can get into a practice room. They don't like trumpet playing at my hotel. I've got an audition at Manhattan on Tuesday. And then one at Juilliard, and another at William Paterson over in New Jersey. Are you studying at Manhattan?"

"No, I'm in high school, a senior. You too?" He nods, and I say, "But my teacher's a professor at Manhattan. And I've got an audition coming up there too. After Juilliard."

He nods slowly. "Welcome to crunch time."

I nod back. "Exactly."

"I'm from Chicago," he says. "How about you?"

"I live two blocks from here. With my grandfather."

"Cool."

I don't mention that I'm actually from West Virginia. On Friday, I'm a New Yorker. Cool.

He takes a last noisy pull on the straw in his empty cup, puts it on the table, stands up, and says, "It was great to see a familiar face. Maybe I'll see you at auditions. My name's Robert. Good to meet you." And he holds out his hand.

I shake it and say, "I'm Gwen. Good to meet you too."

Still holding my hand he says, "I know you're busy, with auditions and everything, but there's a concert tonight at Lincoln Center. And there's an extra ticket. Sorry I can't invite your grandfather too, but do you want to come?"

It's a nice smile. Still, I shake my head. "I really have to practice tonight. But thanks." And I smile back.

His smile gets even nicer, and he shrugs. "No problem. Well, look, I'm at the Empire Hotel, right across from Lincoln Center. And if you change your mind, just call me. The room's under my dad's name, David Phillips. And I'll be there till seven-thirty, okay?"

He still has my hand. I nod. "Okay."

Except there's no way I'm going to miss that much practice time. But I don't let that thought show on my face. I probably look like I might actually say yes, like I might go to Lincoln Center on Friday night with a trumpet player. Who finally lets go of my hand, walks out of the coffee shop, waves, smiles once more, and then heads north on Broadway.

Yeats would probably want to write a poem about this sudden turn in my story. I tuck his book into the pocket on my violin case, leave money on the table, and hurry home to rescue my wilting daffodils. I've got to practice. And eat. And then practice some more.

And I do all that, and the hour of playing before dinner goes well, and the hour after dinner goes even better.

And that's when I decide I deserve some recreation, some culture. Because it's Friday night in New York City. I'm sure Yeats would approve. And Wordsworth.

And so would Grampa. I'm sure he would.

The desk clerk at the Empire Hotel speaks with a Japanese accent. He connects me to the right room, but the line is busy, so after the tone I say, "Robert, it's Gwen, from the coffee shop today. I'll be in the lobby at seven-thirty. Bye."

And then I hurry and shower and dress and dash for the subway. Because I'm going to Lincoln Center. On Friday night. With a trumpet player. Who has a nice smile.

chapter 5

FIELD TRIP

The concert on Friday night isn't quite at Lincoln Center. And it's not the New York Philharmonic playing, which is what I'd expected. The concert is in the Jazz at Lincoln Center complex at Columbus Circle. And the program features Wynton Marsalis and the Lincoln Center Jazz Orchestra.

Robert's parents don't come with us, which seems a little odd. It's just me and the trumpet player. And he actually has his trumpet. I ask why, and he says, "It's a three-thousand-dollar horn, and it's the only one I've got, and it's either lock it up in the hotel safe, or carry it. So I carry it."

Jazz. I don't avoid it, but I don't seek it out. I grew up on bluegrass, and I'm in love with classical now, but I've never gotten into jazz. The next time someone offers free concert tickets, I need to ask for details.

William Paterson University. That's the tip I didn't catch in the coffee shop when Robert listed his auditions. The specialty at William Paterson is jazz. Robert, he of the nice smile, is a jazz trumpeter first, an orchestra player second—but still good enough to get into the Tanglewood classical brass workshop, which is saying something.

And I'm surprised at how much I enjoy the concert. There are fifteen or twenty amazing musicians in the group, and they open with a piece called "Big Train" that Marsalis wrote himself. It's beautifully orchestrated, with a great range of sounds. Our house back home is only half a mile from the Norfolk Southern line, and I know those lonesome train sounds. And feelings.

Some of the other stuff is a little too disjointed for my taste, but Robert loves all the tunes, clapping for every soloist, and he's one of the first people on his feet at the end. The best part for me? I didn't worry about Grampa once for almost two hours.

When Robert first came into the hotel lobby without his parents, it was a surprise, but I don't say anything until after the concert. We're next door to the Empire Hotel eating ice cream—his choice—and it's almost eleven o'clock, just the two of us at a table. Trying to sound casual, I say, "So, how do your parents like the city?"

He shrugs. "They couldn't come. My mom teaches college, and she has midterms, and my dad's locked into a research project. My mom's gonna try to come Thursday, or maybe meet me in Boston next week. They're not real happy about me being a music major anyway."

"How come?"

"Usual reasons—earning a living, job security. Stuff like that."

"Don't they think you're a good musician? I mean, you've got an audition at Juilliard."

"They know I'm talented, but they also know that lots of great musicians never make a good living. And they also know that a big-name school isn't some magic ticket to success. So they worry."

"And you don't?"

Another shrug. "I still want to go for it. It's what I like best, that's all. And my girlfriend thinks I'm really good, and she listens to everything. And my teacher plays in the Chicago Symphony, and he keeps telling me I should go ahead too. So if I can't earn a living in music, then I'll do something else."

My girlfriend. Part of me didn't want to hear that. The part that doesn't want anyone treading on my dreams.

We're done eating, and he says, "I'll ride home with you."

Not a question. A statement.

I shake my head, feeling like I should pull back a little. "You don't have to. Really. There're always lots of people out on a Friday night. I ride the subway alone all the time after the Philharmonic."

He smiles. "Exactly. You get to cruise around New York City all the time, and I don't. So don't spoil my field trip."

Then his face changes. "Aren't we close to where John Lennon got killed?"

I didn't see that coming. "It's about a ten-minute walk."

"Can we go there—would that be okay?"

I nod. "Sure." And we pay our tab, walk out of the restaurant, and start walking uptown.

As many times as I've passed Gray's Papaya at Seventy-second and Broadway, I can never get over the fact that people are always lined up three deep at the counter, day and night. And having stood in line myself a few times, I know why. Even though we're already stuffed with ice cream, I almost insist we each get a papaya and a hot dog. It's one of those must-do things on the Upper West Side.

But I can tell Robert wants to get to the scene of the crime. Seems a little morbid, but also sort of capital-*R* Romantic. Something Paganini might want to do. Or Yeats.

My trumpet player, who has a girlfriend, is full of surprises.

And the next surprise comes when we get to the Dakota, the building where Lennon lived. After we walk past the iron gates where the shooting happened, Robert stops near the corner, opens his case, takes out a silver trumpet, slips a mouthpiece into place, puts a mute in the bell, and begins to play.

The sound has to fight the noise of the traffic on Central Park West, but the melody is warm and strong, and I can hear the words in my mind:

Hey, Jude, don't make it bad.
Take a sad song, and make it better;

I've been to a military funeral, one of my dad's army buddies, and I've been to our town's Memorial Day ceremony every May since I was three. Some buglers can play taps and make you cry, and some can't. Robert can bring the tears.

He goes on with the song, knees bent, eyes closed, and before he's done, ten or twelve other people, all ages, have stopped to listen. When it's over, there are smiles and murmurs, but no applause. It would have been like clapping for the choir in a church.

We walk back toward Broadway, and I say, "That was nice."

He shrugs. "Sort of corny."

"No. Just right." I almost tell him that I'd never be able to do something like that, just take out my instrument and begin playing on a street corner. But it feels too personal. Yes, I'm shy, but why bring it to his attention? I'm too shy to talk about how shy I am.

We talk a little on the subway, mostly about our audition pieces. He's worried most about Haydn, and I'm worried about Paganini.

As we pull out of the 103rd Street station, I remember that I'm going home to another night in an empty house, no Grampa. And I also remember Uncle Hank's little visit before my violin lesson today. And that's when being escorted home begins to feel like an excellent idea.

chapter 6

GWENDOLYN CRUSOE

When we get off the subway at 110th Street, Robert offers to walk me to my door, and I don't argue. Besides, I can tell he's still enjoying his tour of New York at night.

As we wait for a break in the stream of cars and taxis on Broadway, he says, "Unless you're in Old Town, by eleven-thirty Chicago looks pretty empty, even on Friday or Saturday night. New York's a whole different thing." When we're across, he stops to look at the statues lit up by the votive candles that flicker in the window of a bodega. And then he's got his nose against the glass door of the Italian bakery three doors farther south, and he makes me promise we can come again when it's open.

And I'm having fun, just being with someone who's seeing my neighborhood for the first time. Because the variety is wonderful, and I shouldn't take it for granted. I shouldn't take anything for granted.

Once we get to 109th Street, it's a short walk to

Grampa's house. And when I've got the gate and the ground floor door open, and the house feels dark and silent, I say, "Why don't you come in? I'll play you some Paganini if you'll play me some Haydn."

"It's pretty late—think it's okay with your grand-father?"

"It's fine. Really."

I lock the iron gate, and when he's inside, I flip on the hallway lights, lock the door, and set the steel rod back in place.

He nods at the door brace. "We've got an electronic alarm system at my house."

"My grampa says he prefers iron bars and bricks, es-pecially if the power's out."

"Can't argue with that."

When we're upstairs, I can see my daffodils there on the dining table, bright as sunlight. I say, "Want a sand-wich, or something to drink?"

He nods. "Both. Please." He's apparently one of those people who can eat a meal once an hour.

I'm in the kitchen and Robert's walking around the parlor, looking at books, looking at Grampa's war medals, taking in the family photos. "This is you, right? The skinny girl in the middle?"

"Aha—he plays the trumpet, and he's also an expert at flattery."

He grins. "I meant to say, are you the slender brunette with the dimples and the smoky eyes?"

I nod my approval. "Yes, and that's my family. They live in West Virginia, near Charleston."

"Which explains your accent—not what I think of when someone says she lives in New York."

"Accent? What accent?" I say, drawing out the vowels for him.

Maybe it's because I know he has a girlfriend. Maybe that's why I suddenly feel like I can flirt a little. Because that's not like me. But he doesn't know that. At this moment, I think I know more about him than he knows about me.

He flips a thumb toward Grampa's door. "Your granddad's room?" I nod, and he points at the case where Grampa's Purple Heart medal is on display. "He's not going to come charging out here with a bayonet, is he?"

"No chance."

The phone rings on Grampa's desk in the study. It's too late for my mom to call, and I don't want to talk to anyone else. I keep making the sandwich, and Robert says, "You want me to answer that?"

"The machine'll get it." Then I remember again: Every phone call could also be Grampa. And I hold my breath, hoping.

But after the beep it's Uncle Hank, and he's talking so loud, I can hear him from the kitchen.

"Lawrence? . . . Pick up. . . . Blast you, Lawrence! . . . Pick up your phone. . . . Okay, so it's late. But you call me tomorrow at home. I'll be out in the morning, so call me at noon. I tried to call today, and then I come all the way there, and I let myself in to wait, and then Gwen shows up and breathes some fire, and she boots me out—said she'd call your lawyer if I didn't leave. That girl's got some spunk—wonder where she gets that from, huh? Anyway, you call me tomorrow about the house deal, or else I'm gonna have to show up there with the cops . . . so I can check up on my eighty-five-year-old brother who's not answering his phone. This is the wrong time to try to ignore me. And please, tell little Gwennie to stay out of my way, okay? I need that money, Lawrence, do you hear me? I need it. So you call me."

Uncle Hank slams down his phone, there's a dial tone, and the machine shuts off.

Robert looks uncomfortable. He manages a smile and says, "Your grandfather's a sound sleeper."

I put his plate and glass on the table, and as Robert sits down, I tell the truth. "Actually . . . my grampa's not here." Because it seems to me that a person who's not involved, who's just a visitor from Chicago, someone like that would be exempt from what Grampa said. About not telling anybody.

Robert's eyebrows shoot up. "So something *is* going on? Like that guy said?"

I hesitate, then decide. "Can you keep a secret?" Because I want to tell him the rest of it.

His eyes are greenish blue and there's nothing hidden, and he nods. "Keeping secrets is one of my best talents. Right up there with trumpet cadenzas. And flattery."

He follows me into the study with his sandwich and milk. I push the button on the answering machine, and I click back through all of Friday's messages from Uncle Hank, from Kenneth Grant, from Jason the fourth-floor tenant. And I play him Grampa's message from Thursday.

At the part where Grampa says, *Please don't tell anybody I've gone. Especially Hank*, Robert looks at me and nods.

When the message is done, Robert says, "And you don't know when your granddad's coming back?"

"Right."

"And the man who just called, that was Hank?"

"Right again." And then I tell Robert about the invasions and the yelling, and about how they both own the building, and about Uncle Hank being in the house this afternoon.

"He really scared me—and he did it on purpose. He's so . . . inconsiderate." Which wasn't the first word that came to my mind. But I'm trying to do what Grampa said and not judge Uncle Hank. It isn't easy.

"So if you can't reach your grandfather to tell him to call Hank, then he'll use that as an excuse to come blasting in here tomorrow with the police, and then he'll find out his brother is missing, and then he'll take charge of the house. And then little Gwennie will have to go away."

"Exactly," I say. "It's bad timing."

Robert nods. "The worst." And then he's quiet, because he understands how much work, how many years of preparation it's taken me just to get in line for auditions at good music schools—much less get accepted at one. Not to mention get a scholarship.

Then he says, "So what are you going to do?"

"About which part?"

"About your uncle coming here tomorrow. And maybe bringing the police."

I shrug. "There aren't any good choices. And I don't want to start telling a million lies. I should probably just call Grampa's lawyer. He'll know what to do."

Robert shakes his head. "If you do that, then he might go to the police himself if it really looks like a missing-person case. Lawyers are officers of the court."

And I wonder how someone like Robert would know a thing like that. Another surprise from the trumpet man.

Then I have another thought. "But maybe the police *should* be involved. What if my grampa's really in trouble? I have no idea where he is, and I keep imagining the worst. Like, what if he went out yesterday afternoon, and he fell down somewhere, and the police just scooped him up and thought he was a wino, and they took him to Bellevue, or to a jail somewhere?"

Robert looks at me, and his eyes seem so deep and clear. He says, "Well, you should absolutely do whatever you think is best. But on that tape it sounded to me like your grampa knew what he was up to. And it also sounded like he wants you to keep on with your own work. And he wants you to keep Hank in the dark about everything else. So . . ."

Robert's quiet again, and then he says, "Look. You need about two weeks, right? To get done with your auditions?"

"Only half that to finish the most important ones."

"Okay, so you just need to stall your uncle for seven days. And all you're doing is what your grampa asked. He said to keep his house going for him while he's away. This is his place, and you have his permission. His brother can't just whip in here because he leaves for a while. And your grampa left you in charge. Are you eighteen yet?"

I shake my head. "No, seventeen."

Robert wanted a different answer.

"Well," he says, "even if you're a minor, you're still old enough to be left at home without supervision. And you've definitely been left in charge."

"Right," I say, "but Hank's going to stir up trouble, and that's enough to ruin everything. If I can't stay focused on my final prep work, I might as well not even take these auditions. I should just buy a bus ticket and go home."

"Oh, well, that's clearly the winning attitude."

"Don't be sarcastic."

"Then don't talk like a dropout," he snaps. Then, gentler, Robert says, "Look, let me hear that message again."

I point at the machine. "Be my guest."

He ignores the frost in my voice and sits down and plays Grampa's message. Then Robert swivels the chair toward the bookcases and starts to talk, pretending that he's on the phone. "Hank? This is Lawrence. What do you want?" And then he coughs. "Me? I'm fine. I just don't want to talk to you, and that's that. So stop bothering me. Now good-bye."

I stare at him, and my mouth is hanging open because Robert is using Grampa's voice—not perfect, but really close.

I say, "How did you *do* that?"

"Gwennie? Is that you? I need you to keep the house going for me while I'm away."

"*Quit* it! How did you learn to *do* that?"

He grins at me. "Mostly from this stupid game I play with my girlfriend. When we're out, like maybe to eat or at the mall, sometimes I try to make her think someone else is talking to her. It's gonna sound sick, because she's actually blind."

My mouth is hanging open again. "Your girlfriend's *blind*? Really? And you trick her? With fake voices? That *is* sick."

He's laughing now. "No, but it's not, not for us. It's just a game—really. And when I start using some new voice, sometimes she knows it's me, but she pretends she doesn't know, and she goes along with it, and then *she* zaps me. And sometimes I get everything perfect, and she really thinks I'm somebody else. And sometimes I do it when I call her on the phone. So I'm in practice. And I am completely *awesome* at prank phone calls. So I think your grampa needs to give mean old Hank a call. Tomorrow about noon."

His cell phone rings, and I jump a mile. Robert takes a look and says, "It's Alicia—that's her, my girlfriend."

So I nod and leave the study, pulling the door shut behind me. I can hear him talking, then laughing. And I can picture his smile.

Nothing's really changed here. Grampa's still missing, Uncle Hank is still yelling, and my auditions are one day closer. But I feel better anyway. I don't know if Robert can help me or not, but I do believe that he really wants to try. And I don't feel like I'm on my own anymore, at least not the way I was this morning.

So many surprises.

On Friday, a little before midnight, I realize that instead of those poems by Yeats, I ought to be rereading *Robinson Crusoe*. Because that's more like my story—me, alone on an island. Manhattan is not a tropical paradise, but Grampa's ship is lost at sea, and Uncle Hank is doing a good job playing the part of a hostile native. And me, I'm the castaway.

In Defoe's novel, Robinson Crusoe finds a helper, and he names him Friday. And the castaway is sure that this helper has been sent to him by divine Providence.

So if I'm Gwendolyn Crusoe, then maybe Robert is going to be my man Friday.

Who has a girlfriend.

chapter 7

BUYING TIME

F riday night ends when Robert leaves around one A.M., and before he goes, we've got a plan. I walk him to the door, and he says, "You sure you're okay here? Alone and everything?" And the look on his face makes me think he wouldn't enjoy it, himself.

"Me? Sure. I'm fine. And the place has great locks. Very secure."

"Good. So, I'll see you tomorrow." And he's gone. Because I've convinced him that I've got everything under control.

But once I'm ready for bed, Gwen the brave one seems to be missing in action. This house is older than my violin, and the place breathes and creaks and clanks, especially when the furnace goes on and off during the night. I finally get to sleep by locking the door of my room and leaving the closet light on, and then saying the twenty-third psalm to myself about fifteen times. But I still have bad dreams, except now they're about Grampa.

. . .

As we planned, Robert comes back to the Page family brownstone around eleven on Saturday morning, still carrying his trumpet, and I've got some chocolate croissants and fresh orange juice ready for our breakfast.

It's another bright February day, warmer than normal. I'm warmer than normal too. I can't quite believe what Robert's going to do, and I'm feeling feverish.

After we eat and then sit in the parlor reading the Saturday paper awhile, it's still about twenty minutes until noon. So I say, "Bring your trumpet and I'll show you my practice room."

He picks up the padded case and follows me to the ground floor where I left my violin, and then we go downstairs to my studio.

"This is great."

He's right. It's not a big space, but the lighting is good, and the acoustics are perfect.

"My grampa had it built special. First he drove the carpenter crazy, then the electrician, and then the painter. It's my favorite place in the whole world."

"And no one can hear you play down here?"

"No one," I say, "at least not the violin."

"Then it's time to give it the trumpet test. Better shut the door."

He sets up his horn, and with no warm-up, he takes off into the last movement of the Haydn trumpet concerto. It's all from memory, clean and classical, a silver river—almost five minutes with no letup. And it's very good.

And then, effortlessly, he's playing a jazz solo, something I think I've heard before. And it's cool and glassy on the surface, hot and liquid underneath. He leans into the notes, fingers on the pearl buttons, turning the air different shades of blue. It could almost change the way a girl feels about jazz.

Before he stops, I have my violin out, and as he finishes, I cut in with the runs from the middle of caprice number 17. It's his turn to listen. And having watched him so closely, now I'm aware of every move *I* make, each dip of my shoulder and slash of the bow. And I know Robert's watching my fingers dance the way I watched his.

And I get so flustered that I have to stop.

He says, "No, keep going—please."

I'm blushing, and I say, "Could you maybe not look right at me when I play? It makes me nervous. It's . . . it's a problem I have. I hate playing solos, and if I ever get the orchestra job I want, I'll never have to play solos. But you know how it works. Because before I get that job, I'll have to do a jillion auditions. And every audition means I have to play a solo. So it's a problem."

He nods. "I was like that, scared to be out front. I'm playing with the jazz band, and Mr. Stojis points at me to take a solo, and the drums and the piano have this great rhythm cooking, and I lift up my horn . . . and nothing comes out but little squeaks. Happened over and over. Pitiful."

Remembering the way he played for John Lennon, I say, "But you're not shy now. Because I saw you last night, right there with people all around us. So how'd you get over it?"

This unsettled look zips across his face, just for a second, and then Robert leans toward me and he says, "The truth? A couple years ago . . . I mean . . . well, no. It's a really long story."

He smiles, then looks down and clicks the valve buttons on his horn. It's the first time I've seen him look flustered.

And once again I have the feeling that my trumpet player is full of surprises. Plus a secret or two.

Then he says, "But let's try something." And he reaches over and flips off the light. Which is, in fact, another surprise.

This room is fifteen feet underground, with a double-thick door and no windows. Complete darkness.

And Robert's voice says, "Now. Just play."

"Is . . . is this what you did, play in the dark? To stop feeling shy?"

"Sort of. But don't talk. Just play."

And then another thought, a big one. "Is it because your girlfriend's blind, is that it? The darkness?"

"Just play, okay?"

So I do. I take a deep breath, and then the burst of

notes that starts the caprice comes winging out of nowhere, filling the space. The staccato runs, the sharp double-stops, the rush and the flutter and the punch, and it's all as if the music is happening without me.

My fingers love the dark. They know where they need to be, and they know what they need to do. And this piece sounds so strong. The music is powerful, and so am I, here alone in the dark.

But I know I'm not alone. Robert's three feet away. Or three miles. Hard to tell.

I'm still playing, whipping my bow from string to string, slashing toward the end, and now I understand why he did it, why Robert shut off the light: So he'd disappear. And me too. Because that's what needs to happen, with or without the light. You have to let yourself disappear.

After the Paganini, it's still for a moment. Then, because I truly am from West Virginia, I make my violin speak like a fiddle, and I begin playing "The Water Is Wide." It's an ancient tune, deep and dignified. After one verse, his trumpet reaches out and takes the melody, so I weave a simple harmony through the inky air, first high and then from beneath.

The folk song ends, and the silence is dense and peaceful. I have not felt so much at home in a long time.

Out of the darkness, he says, "Nice."

And I whisper, "Very nice."

And then sitting in the dark suddenly seems too weird, so I fumble for the lights, and as we both blink and smile, I say, "Your teacher's right. And your girl-friend. You really are good."

"You too."

"Thanks."

He dries out his trumpet and puts it away. And as I pack up my bow and fiddle, I love my practice room even more.

Then Robert looks at his watch and says, "It's show time."

I'm following him up the stairs toward the parlor, and I say, "Do you really think we should do this? I mean, couldn't we get in trouble?"

He stops and turns to look down at me from the top step. "I don't think there's much risk. And getting your uncle to back off for a week or so doesn't seem wrong— not at all. You're just trying to keep the house going for your grampa. Which is what he asked you to do, re-member? And I know just what I'm going to say. I'm not going to tell any lies. I'm going to make simple, true statements. And I'm going to use an old-man voice. So it's like I'm making a prank call. And what Hank de-cides to make of it, well, that's his business."

I shake my head. "Some smart attorney would love to hear you say all that—and then she'd tear you up into tiny bits and feed you to a judge."

Turning and walking into the study, Robert says, "If everything works out right, that'll never happen. I'm ready to dial." Then using Grampa's voice, he says, "Now where's that darned telephone number?"

I can't bear to stay in the study, so I pace back and forth in the parlor. It's not a speakerphone, so I can only hear Robert's half of the conversation. He sounds exactly like Grampa.

"Hello? . . . Well, that's none of your business. . . . You can think whatever you want to. . . . Gwennie? She's doing just what she's supposed to do. . . . Can't help that. . . . Well, go ahead and think whatever you want to. But don't come around here. You want to talk, talk to my lawyer."

Then Robert lets loose with a big coughing fit, and when he's done, he says, "And that's the end of it. . . . No, that's the end of it."

And then he hangs up.

I'm back in the study, and I'm looking at Robert's face. He tries a smile, but it doesn't work. His cheeks are flushed.

"That guy sounds totally out of it today—yelling and swearing, and he says he's got papers all ready to sign. And he says he needs to borrow some money against his half of this house or he's going to lose his business. And he needs to get it settled right now. No wonder your grandfather wanted to get away."

I shake my head. "If you're saying Grampa ran away and left me to deal with all this because he was afraid or something, that's not true—that's not like him at all. You saw those war medals in the parlor. He would never run from a fight."

Robert says, "Okay, but if he knew Hank was so nuts

about needing some money, and he knew Hank was going to keep pushing, then why do *you* think your grandfather left all of a sudden?"

That stops me cold. But then the answer comes to me so clearly. "Grampa must have been pretty sure that if he'd stayed, things would have been worse."

"Worse than this?" Robert makes a face. "How?"

I shrug and I say, "I don't know."

And on Saturday, that's true. I don't know how things could be worse. But I'm sure Grampa wouldn't have made it hard for me, not on purpose.

And then I think, Wouldn't it be nice if everything always happened on purpose.

And then I think, Maybe it does.

chapter 8

HOUSEGUEST

After the phone call to Uncle Hank we have some lunch before we each spend about two hours practicing down in my studio, me first and then Robert.

And then late Saturday afternoon I ask him about staying the night.

"I mean, if you want to. You could even check out of your hotel and just stay here until your auditions are done. In Grampa's room. If it's okay with your mom and dad. And you can practice here anytime you want to."

I keep myself from saying that I don't want to spend another night alone in this house. But I think he knows that.

He smiles and nods. "That'd be great. And my folks'll like it, me being at someone's house instead of a hotel—staying with this kid I know from Tanglewood." Robert's already composing what he's going to say to his parents.

And he leaves and comes back at about six-thirty

with a rolling suitcase and a backpack and a bag of Chinese food. Which is good, because I'm famished.

After we've each wolfed down some egg rolls and chicken with pea pods, I ask, "So what did your parents say? When you told them about staying here."

He keeps busy with his chopsticks, talking between bites. "My dad was fine with it, but then my mom said she wanted to talk to your grandfather, and I told her that he's away for a while. And then she got all mothered out. So I just said, Well, this is what I'm doing because I'm sure it's all right, and if you were here, you'd know it was all right too. But you're *not* here, so you'll have to take my word for it. And I checked out of the Empire, and here I am."

When we're done eating, he says, "So who's got the practice room first tonight, you or me? I don't mind taking the late shift."

Which is perfect for me, because I had the early practice this afternoon, and I'm ready to take another run at my pieces, especially the Bach partitas.

I'm at the top of the stairs when Robert says, "Have you ever played a fiddle tune for your teacher at Manhattan? Because you should."

I make a face. "Bad idea. Pyotr Melyanovich would not be amused. He's *very* formal."

"Doesn't mean he won't like it. Because you should be using that, the energy and the feelings. Have you heard a CD called *Appalachian Journey*?"

I shake my head. "Bluegrass?"

"It's Yo-Yo Ma with Mark O'Connor on violin and Edgar Meyer on bass, all three of them classical geniuses. And you should hear what they do with a bunch of old melodies."

"And you're saying—"

"That it flows both ways. Classical training is great, but there's stuff way back in the mountains that's just as important. Ask Bartok. Ask Sibelius. They know about folk music. I'm just saying you should use everything you've got. And your teacher would say the same thing. Unless he's an idiot. End of lecture."

I nod and say, "Thank you, professor."

And he grins and bows stiffly.

As I walk down to my practice room, I have to admit it's good advice. Because it's like I have one head that's filled with fiddle tunes and denim overalls, and a newer head that's all sheet music and crystal chandeliers and people wearing tuxedos and evening gowns. And sometimes I still feel like I have to stop being my old self when I play classical music.

But this is not a problem I want to tackle tonight. Tonight I have a different task.

At the bottom of the basement steps I imagine that it's Tuesday morning. I'm walking along a hallway at Juilliard. Because I'm pretending that I'm actually taking my first audition.

I walk into the room and close the door behind me. I prepare my bow and violin and test the tuning. I nod respectfully at each of the faculty members, and I imagine what they ask me to play first. Then I look briefly up at the ceiling to clear my mind, and I begin. And suddenly I'm also imagining that the lights have clicked off, that no one can see me. And it helps. It's only the music. And I don't stop for anything. I play.

Getting into college is different for a music student. It's not just, What were your grades? And it's not, Which clubs did you belong to, and Were you the class president? And it's not, What are your SAT scores?

The question for a music student is so simple, only three words: Can you play? Can you walk into this audition room and play—today, right now—without messing up?

And you only get one chance to get it right because that's how you have to play music in the real world, in a performance. You practice and practice and rehearse, and when it's time for the performance, you come onstage and take your place. Then the conductor raises the baton and nods, and if you don't come in on the right beat with the right notes and the right pitch and the right attack, then you've let down the conductor, and you've let down the other ninety-five musicians in the orchestra, and you've let down the audience. And, of course, you've stabbed your bow straight through the heart of the composer. Because the only question is, Can you play?

On Saturday night I feel confident, and it's good rehearsal time, almost two hours, with Sibelius winning the prize for my most improved composer, and Paganini a close second.

When I come back up to the parlor, Robert is sitting in Grampa's recliner, eyes closed, head tipped back, with his earbuds in and his iPod resting on the arm of the chair. I tiptoe over and look at the little screen to see what he's listening to: *Kind of Blue*. It's Miles Davis— jazz. And I remind myself that sometime I have to ask Robert how he connects his jazz with his classical playing. Because I'm sure he's got a theory about that. I've known him less than two days, and it's already perfectly clear that Robert has at least one theory about everything in the universe.

I touch him on the shoulder, and he jumps like he's been half asleep, and it takes him a second to recognize me. He pulls out the earphones and I say, "Your turn. To practice."

"Great," and Robert gets out of the chair and heads downstairs.

First I finish loading the dinner dishes into the dishwasher, and then I put clean sheets and pillowcases on Grampa's bed, and open a window to air out the room. As I put clean towels in the bathroom, that's when I notice that Grampa didn't take his hairbrush and comb. Or his toothbrush and electric razor. Which seems odd, that he'd leave in that much of a hurry.

And right away I want to try to figure out what it

might mean. Of course, it might just mean that he decided to take one of those plastic disposable razors instead of the electric one, and that he took one of the new toothbrushes that his dentist always gives him. And who knows how many combs and brushes he owns? Or it could be that since he was in a hurry, Grampa just forgot. Everybody forgets stuff.

Even though I can find all these perfectly logical explanations, my worries follow me around like a dark swarm of bees. And I run to the creek, and I dive down deep, and I hold my breath as long as I can. But when I come up, gasping for air, I can still hear the buzzing.

And once again I try to take some shelter in Grampa's last order to me: *You just keep about your own business and leave all the worrying to me.*

Grampa and his orders. My dad said that time in the army does that to a man, makes him think like a soldier for the rest of his life, especially if he's been to war.

I finish my chores and then I curl up on the couch with my book of poems. But I get up after a few minutes and go into the study. I roll Grampa's desk chair out of the way, and I reach up and pull *Pride and Prejudice* off the shelf. For the third time. Because tonight doesn't feel like a Yeats night. This is a Jane Austen night.

And I turn to go back to the parlor, but I stop. Because I can hear something. There's music playing. And at first I think it's a radio from upstairs.

But it's not. It's Robert. I pull out the chair and sit

down, and I can hear the slow movement of the Haydn trumpet concerto drifting up out of the metal vent on the floor. It's not loud, but it's clear.

The music is beautiful, but that's not why my eyes fill up with tears. It's because I never knew. Grampa could have had the carpenter block every bit of sound from below. But he didn't. He saved some. For himself. Just a little, so he could sit here when he wanted to and listen to me play my violin. And I never knew.

I smile when Robert ends the movement with a long fluttering trill, and then I wipe my eyes and carry *Pride and Prejudice* back into the parlor. I lie down again on the couch, and I open the book and begin to read.

But on this particular Saturday night, I ask myself, Why do I like this book so much?

Because someone could read this book and think that it's just a sappy story about this girl and her sisters, and how they're all trying so desperately to get married, to find the men who will save them from being old maids.

Truth: I have given no serious time in my life to love and romance. Almost zero. Since seventh grade I have never dreamed of anything except becoming a great violinist in a great orchestra. And even now, that's still my top priority.

But here I am, reading *Pride and Prejudice* again.

I flip ahead until I find the last chapter, and after reading a page or two, I realize that it's the main character, Elizabeth. She's the reason I love this book. Lizzy is smart, and she's not just going along with what everyone expects her to do. And she's got everyone figured out, except Mr. Darcy. And herself. But that comes full circle by the end.

And I love Jane Austen's use of language too—the way she takes her time to develop a phrase and gives it room to grow, so that these clever, complex statements form slowly and then bloom in my mind. Beethoven does the same thing with his cadence and phrasing and structure. It's a fact: Jane Austen is musical. And so's Yeats. And Wordsworth. All the great writers are musical.

Thank you again, Miss Page, for more brilliant literary insights.

When Robert comes back upstairs, I don't tell him that I listened to him playing from the study. That's a secret, mine and Grampa's.

Robert and I serve ourselves some ice cream, chocolate for him, vanilla for me. We turn on the tube and catch some *Saturday Night Live*, but I'm too worn-out to keep my eyes open.

"I've got to sleep now."

Eyes on the screen, Robert says, "Okay. See you tomorrow." Then he turns and smiles. "And thanks for asking me to stay. This is really great."

I nod. "For me too."

And I go downstairs and get ready for bed, and before I close my door, I listen at the bottom of the stairs. I don't hear the TV, so I call, "Good night."

But Robert must be in Grampa's room already, because he doesn't answer.

So I shut my door and lie down and turn off the light.

Then I count my blessings.

And the last thing I do is say a prayer for my grampa.

And I hope that he has a nice new toothbrush.

chapter 9

MODULATION

I sleep until ten on Sunday morning, and when I go upstairs to the kitchen, Robert's already there reading the *Times*, and then he makes breakfast for both of us, scrambled eggs and toast.

"So what should we do today?" he says. "I mean, besides practicing? Want to go out for a while?"

I shrug. "It looks like a decent day. I'd be happy with a walk along the Hudson or something. Or do you want to be a real tourist—Statue of Liberty? Empire State Building? Something like that?"

He shakes his head. "No, that's too much. But I do need some new running shoes. And I've heard that the New York Niketown store is pretty cool. How's that for excitement?"

"Sounds fine."

I call the store to check their hours. The place is open until seven, and we decide there's enough time for each of us to practice for an hour before we go. So we do, because we're both such insanely responsible young musicians.

Then it's a subway ride down to Columbus Circle.

I love to watch people in New York, but if you make eye contact with the wrong person, it can get scary. Like the woman who was singing her own opera on a bus one afternoon. I was new in town, and I smiled and nodded at her, and suddenly the lady stands up and points, and begins singing at the top of her lungs. About me:

This child, this child of deadly Zeus,
She brings ruin and destruction down upon
　our heads.
Shun her, shun her, fear her evil eye,
For she has sold her soul to the bloodred moon.

Her performance ran for more than thirty blocks, and all the time my face was beet-red because everyone was looking at me. And when I got off, the lady rushed to the back of the bus and kept singing at me out the window.

Stuff like that can make a deep impression on a young newcomer to the big city.

So now I do my people-watching in quick glances, and in our subway car I don't spot anyone who grabs my imagination. In fact, Robert and I may be the most interesting people around at the moment. Everybody else is probably watching us.

And as I think this, I notice that I'm enjoying sitting next to Robert. And I realize that when people see us sitting like this, they might think we're together, that he's my boyfriend. And suddenly I feel like Lizzy in *Pride*

❧

and Prejudice, and Robert is Mr. Darcy, and I'm writing Robert into my story, imagining what the two of us would be like as a couple.

The thought makes me blush, and to punish myself I say, "So tell me about your girlfriend—you said her name's Alicia?"

He nods and gets this smile on his face, a sweet one I haven't seen yet. "Right, Alicia. Well, she's real, real smart. And she's a great writer, and we like reading the same kind of books. We listen to a lot of music, and she's heard me play my trumpet more than anyone else on the planet. And I'm not kidding—she is not afraid of *anything*. Makes me feel like a wimp."

The train stops at Seventy-second Street, and our conversation is interrupted by the noise of twenty people getting off and thirty others getting on.

When we're moving again, I say, "Do you have a picture of her?"

He shakes his head. "Not even one. I know that sounds strange, but she's never seen me at all, what I look like. So I keep her pictures in my head, like she does. I mean, she's really pretty and everything. It's just not why I like her."

I let that sink in. And now I'm really curious. "Doesn't it bother you sometimes, like, that you can't go see a movie together? And do other stuff?"

He shakes his head. "We watch DVDs all the time. I describe what's going on right while it's happening. I'm a genius at it. So I get to watch the movie, and I also get to watch her face as I tell her about it. It's the best. And if you've never been the guide for a blind person who's riding a bike in front of you, it's an experience. I mean, we only do that at night in this museum parking lot. It's huge and flat, and all I have to do is keep her from hitting the light poles. And we work out at a gym together, and we've been camping and kayaking—even skiing on some little hills up in Wisconsin. So it's not like we don't do stuff. It's just different, that's all." I can only imagine how different it would be. Like learning to see the world all over again. Or maybe like learning how to play the violin in the dark.

We get off at the Fifty-ninth Street station at the bottom of Central Park, walk down Broadway to Fifty-seventh Street, and then go east. He wants to go into the big bookstore on the corner, and normally, so would I. But I'm watching the time. I really do want to get back to my practice room, so I suggest that we save that pleasure for some other trip.

A block later, I've got a surprise for him, but he sees it before I can tell him.

"Hey, look—Carnegie Hall! *Everybody's* played there—even Miles Davis."

And watching Robert's face, I remember the first time I saw the place, all lit up at night, with banners announcing a performance by Yo-Yo Ma. At this moment it looks more like a drab hotel than the world's most famous concert hall. A glass and metal marquee reaches out over the sidewalk, and if the fancy old bronze poster frames weren't hanging on either side of the doorways, it would be easy to walk right past the place. My teacher told me that his namesake, Pyotr Ilich Tchaikovsky, was the conductor at the very first concert here in 1891. And when I told my uncle Belden that I'd actually attended a performance at Carnegie Hall, he said, "So, what, is it like the Grand Ole Opry?" And I told him, "Yes—in a way, I guess it is."

After we hike east and cross Fifth Avenue, the Nike store's right there, and unlike Carnegie Hall, there's no way to miss it. The façade is mostly polished granite, and there's this huge arched window that goes up and up. It's not your everyday shoe store at the mall, which is the full extent of my relationship with footwear. This place is more like an athletics theme park, or a high-tech Greek temple that specializes in foot worship. We wander around for almost an hour, just gawking at the plastic and the polished metal and the wall-sized graphics of the sports gods, plus all the multimedia displays— five floors of it. And then Robert finally picks out a pair of ridiculously expensive running shoes. After he pays, we start to head for the exit on the far side of the atrium.

Suddenly Robert stops, so I stop too. He's looking at something, and I turn my head to see, but he steps around in front of me. "No, don't stare."

"What? Stare at what?" Because from the look on his face I'm thinking it's got to be Michael Jordan himself. Or maybe a vampire.

He's talking to me in a rushed whisper. "Okay, look

at the tile wall, to the left of the Tiger Woods poster. No, don't. Don't point. And try not to stare. Just take a quick look at the wall and tell me what you see. Because I think I see something there."

So I look, and there is something. I say, "There's . . . sort of a shadow, except it's not very dark, and it's kind of blurry—but . . . it's a man's shadow."

He nods, agreeing. "Okay. And do you see how his shadow's moving?"

"Yeah—the guy keeps turning his head. I mean the shadow. It's blurry, but it looks like he's got a lot of hair. And a beard."

"Okay," Robert says, "that's the shadow. Now, locate the person who's making the shadow."

I look around, trying to be casual about it. From the hair and the beard in the shadow, I'm thinking to spot a hippie, or maybe some homeless guy with dreadlocks.

There's an older woman with an umbrella and a canvas shopping bag. And a young mom with a baby in a stroller. I see two teenage girls wearing black leather jackets, and ten or twelve college guys, all with short hair, and most of them tall—looks like a whole basketball team. And lots of other people. But no long-haired, bearded guys—not near, not far, not on the first or the second floor, not anywhere.

And I turn to glance at the guy's shape again, and suddenly the shadow wiggles, and it's gone. Just gone.

The hairs on the back of my neck tingle, and I say, "What . . . what *was* that?"

Robert whispers, "Probably nothing. Let's go."

But I can tell he's spooked.

And that feeling I've had, that Robert is full of surprises? It's not just a feeling anymore. And as we rush out of the store, I'm wondering if it was really a good idea to invite him to stay at Grampa's with me.

We're out on the street, and I have to trot to keep up with him, and when we cross the Avenue of the Americas, I say, "Hey, you can slow down. I just looked, and the shadow isn't chasing us."

He snaps, "Not funny."

He's really upset, so I say, "Sorry. I just . . . I mean, I don't know what's happening . . . I don't know what that was about."

Still walking fast, still snapping, he says, "That's right. You don't know."

"So tell me." But he doesn't say anything, and he doesn't slow down.

When we get to Carnegie Hall, I say, "I have to catch my breath," and I find a place under the marquee that's not covered with pigeon droppings, and I sit on the low step with my back against the glass in the second doorway. In the shade it feels ten degrees colder, and even though I'm overheated, I shiver.

Robert sits beside me, and he's breathing hard too. After a minute or so he says, "Remember how you asked me if I could keep a secret?" I nod, and he says, "So, how about you? Can you keep one?"

"Yes, I can. I will."

He nods, but he doesn't say anything. And I get ready, because I have no idea what's coming. He's watching the traffic, so I'm looking at one side of his face, and he's thinking hard. Finally he says, "Okay. What would you say if I told you that two years ago I turned invisible?"

I want to laugh, but looking at his face, I know not to. "In . . . visible? You mean, for real? Like, no one could see you?"

He nods, still looking at the cars and taxis going by. "Right. No one could see me for almost a month. Because my body stopped reflecting light. For real. What would you say if I told you that?"

"*Is* that what you're telling me?"

"Just answer my question. What would you say? If I told you that."

"Well . . . if I believed you, or if I just wanted to go along with the story, I'd say, So how did this happen?"

He nods and says, "And if you asked me that, I'd say, It was because of scientific principles—spectroscopic anomalies, particle light theory—physics, stuff I don't completely understand. But it really happened, and some other people saw it happen the same way I did, a whole group of very smart, very normal people. It happened to me, but they saw it too. So it wasn't my imagination, and we can't all be crazy. That's what I'd say back to you. If you went along with the first part."

"About becoming invisible," I say.

"Right."

Of course, I'm not going along with the first part because it's got to be some kind of a joke, but I'm nodding anyway. I feel like I've edged my way out onto a frozen pond, and the ice isn't thick enough, so I want to stop . . . but it's not safe to stand still, either. So I take another step. Because I have to.

And I say, "So if we got this far, I guess my next question would be, Who are these other people, the ones who know for sure that this really happened to you?"

Robert glances at my face, then looks beyond me, scanning the flow of people walking toward us. And I see a tiny flicker of fear in his eyes, there and gone. Then he turns back to watching the cars. He smiles to himself and says, "That's the right question. Who else knows? And to answer you, I'd say, there's my mom, who teaches literature at the University of Chicago; there's my dad, who's a physicist at the Fermi National Lab; there's Alicia's mom, a serious, college-educated American citizen; and there's Alicia's dad, also a physicist and also a professor at U of C. And there's Alicia. And now, you."

He looks at me. I'm trying to keep my face still, trying not to let my thinking show. But he sees I'm confused. And he probably sees I'm also a little scared. And I am. Because, really, I don't know this boy. For all I know, he's got serious problems.

He turns back and stares up at the buildings across the street. "It's okay if you don't believe me. But keep all that a secret anyway. Because it's not a story. And there's more. While we were working out the problem two years ago, I found someone else. Another person it happened to. Only one—but it was important because that proved it didn't only happen to me. And that's what I think we saw back there. In the Nike store. Another one."

And suddenly my heart's beating so fast, it's hard to breathe, and my mind is stuttering at itself—*N-no! N-no way!*

Because I don't know what to think. Because I really did see it. That shadow. A faint, wavy shadow of a guy with long hair, turning his head, looking around, there in the store, up against the wall. I saw it. His shadow was there, but there wasn't a body to match it. And then his shadow disappeared. Just vanished. I saw it.

Robert stands and brushes off his pants. "Ready?" And he reaches down to help me. And when I look up into his face and take his hand, that's when I start to believe. This person pulling me to my feet is not a liar. And he's not weird, not at all. And I'm not afraid of him, or of what he's saying. Because why would he make up a story like that? And I *did* see it. That shadow. I saw it with my own eyes. I saw it.

Riding the subway home, he answers my questions, and I have a lot of them. Because once I accept that any of his story is even a tiny bit possible, I want to know everything, all the details. And he tells me everything, except he doesn't tell me what triggered the phenomenon. That's what he calls it—the phenomenon.

"And you . . . you went out in public too?"

He nods, and I say, "But, like . . . you couldn't wear clothes, right?"

He nods again, blushing now. "Yup. Naked as a Greek statue. Takes some getting used to."

He tells me how he stood out in front of his high school, watching the kids come out after school. And how he took a long cab ride with Alicia. Naked.

As I listen, I'm still trying to find a reason to dismiss the whole thing as crazy, but the story's tight. There's nothing inconsistent, nothing off-key. Because it's like when I begin to play my violin: If one string is even a little out of tune, it can't be hidden. And I hear Robert's voice and I see his eyes, and there's not a single false note.

Sitting on the noisy, swaying train, I begin struggling with the idea that someone could be hidden like that. I look around at all the people. And I'm trying to imagine what it would be like to be invisible. For a month. Even if I don't completely believe it happened, I believe that Robert believes it did. I'm sure of that much.

And then I have this sudden mind-snap, and I know what Robert didn't tell me the other night. In my practice room, about how he got over being shy. He had *this* experience. Two years ago. And it was like disappearing. Shutting off the lights.

And even though I don't know what to believe, I'm also sure I really saw that shadow man—or at least something that *looked* like a man's shadow. And I wonder where that guy is right now. If he's real, that is . . . if

I really saw what I think I saw. Or if I really saw what Robert thinks I saw.

And I steal a look at Robert, and I try to imagine what effects being invisible might have had on him. If it happened. Because an experience like that would have to leave some marks. If it happened.

And then I steal a look at myself, at my reflection in the window on the other side of the subway car. And I wonder what the experience of just *knowing* about this stuff is going to have on me—even if it's only knowing that Robert believes it happened.

Because I can already feel a change in the way I look at people. And at myself. And it's also changed the way I look at Robert, and not just because of *the phenomenon*. I'm seeing him differently because of the way he's taken me into his confidence. That took some courage. After the thing in the Nike store, he could have just laughed it off, or he could have clammed up. But he chose to tell me. He's trusting me. And I don't want that to stop.

Because I want to keep being friends with Robert. I admit that to myself. I really like him. Not necessarily in a romantic way, or even a Romantic way. I like him in a classical way.

So here I am: My grandfather is a missing person, the most important auditions of my life begin the day after tomorrow, and I'm sitting on the subway next to a boy named Robert who has become my current best friend, and who is easily the most interesting person I've met in years. He's a great musician, he's an original thinker, he's a fearless problem solver. And—oh yes—he's saying that what I saw in the Nike store this afternoon was an invisible man. And what makes Robert think that? Because he was invisible himself for a month or so a few years back. That's what he's telling me.

And even though I've only known Robert for two days, I believe him. And I believe him because I can see that if I'm going to stay friends with him, then I need to accept that what he's told me is true, accept that it happened the way he says it did. And I am willing to do that. I *want* to believe him.

Because it's sort of like this girl at my junior high, Belinda, who said she wanted to tell me a secret. It was at her house one afternoon, and she made me swear on the Bible that I wouldn't tell, and then she told me that she'd been abducted by aliens. And either it really happened to her or else she's a crazy liar, because her story was pretty amazing. So Belinda took a risk, and she told me, and after I listened to her stories, I decided I'd just go along with her. Because, well, why not? Why call someone a liar and lose a friend over something that's impossible to prove or disprove, especially when it'll never have anything to do with my own life? Because this girl wasn't crazy, and she'd never lied about anything else.

And that's sort of how it is with Robert's story. I can accept it because I want to stay friends with Robert, and it won't cost me anything to accept it, because it's just a story, *his* story. It's just something that he says happened to him, and he's shared it with me. But it's not part of *my* life, not really. It's his story, not mine.

Except I never saw Belinda's aliens. And I did see that shadow in the Nike store. So that's different.

We get off at 110th Street and start walking home on Sunday afternoon, and I feel like my world is changing. Again. And there's nothing subtle about it. Everything has shifted, like when a symphony suddenly modulates to a different key.

And I wonder how many times the world can change in one week.

I'm beginning to think that it's a large number.

chapter 10

IMPROVISATION

W̶e're out of the subway, walking south on Broadway, not talking. I glance into the faces of all these people out for a Sunday stroll, but I'm not seeing eyes and noses and mouths. I'm seeing stories. Every person has a story. All the hopes and dreams. And fears. And secrets.

In every face.

So many stories. And I feel like I can't ignore them anymore.

And then I remind myself that I have to keep telling myself my own story. *My* story. Because if I don't, then my story's going to get swallowed up by Grampa's story and Uncle Hank's story. And now Robert's story.

And I remind myself that my story is very simple: I am a musician. I play the violin. That's all I want to do. I am trying to get into music school. I am trying to keep on my practice schedule. I am not concerned with jointly owned buildings, and feuds between brothers, and trumpet players with blind girlfriends. Or some invisible bearded guy at a sporting goods store. Those are all bits and pieces from other people's stories. Not *my* story. I have a job to do here. I've got to get a scholarship to a great music school, and everything else is just a distraction. An obstacle. Because on Tuesday morning I have to walk into a room and face the experts with my borrowed violin and prove that I can play the thing. I have to keep working on *my* story.

This is what I'm saying to myself on Sunday afternoon. And as Robert and I walk along, getting closer to home, I resolve that nothing is going to pull my own narrative off track. Nothing. I am a musician. End of story.

Then Robert and I are less than half a block from Grampa's brownstone, and I stop and I grab the sleeve of his jacket.

"Quick, in here!" And I pull him into the doorway of a dry-cleaning shop.

"What?"

"My uncle—he just went up the front steps." I peek around the edge of the shop window, and Uncle Hank is putting his key into the lock. Then he's in the front hall, and I say, "Let's go—run!"

In ten seconds I'm fumbling with my keys, then we're under the stoop, and then we're inside the ground floor door.

I can hear Uncle Hank upstairs, pounding on the parlor door. And yelling. "Lawrence! Open up! I know you're in there. Open the door!"

I checked the perimeter before we left. I know he can't get in—unless he's got a sledgehammer. But he's making a huge racket, and the tenants and the neighbors are getting an earful.

I put a finger to my lips, and Robert nods and then follows me as I creep up the stairs and into the parlor.

"Lawrence! Open the door. We have to talk." He bangs on the door again, and the heavy panels shake on their hinges. I wish the wood were six inches thicker.

Then Robert walks right over to about three feet from the door, and he says, "I told you yesterday. I don't want to talk about this. Talk to the lawyers. And you're disturbing the peace. So stop shouting and go away."

Robert's using Grampa's voice, leaning forward with his shoulders hunched like an old man.

I press my hands to my cheeks and try not to gasp, but there's no chance of that. I'm so scared, I can't take a breath.

In a much quieter voice Uncle Hank says, "Finally— now open the door so we can talk."

Robert shakes his head. "I don't want to, and I'm not going to."

"Come on, Lawrence." Hank sounds like he's talking to a small child. "Listen, I'm sorry I yelled at you on Thursday. And all that stuff I said, I didn't mean it. I'm sorry. I don't want to put you into a nursing home some-where. You're my big brother, and I care about you. But you have to be reasonable. This building was left to both of us. And I need my share of it now. I need it now. Just let me use the place as collateral. For a loan. That's all I want. You can still live here, and I can get some cash. What's wrong with that? I need the money, Lawrence. How many times do I have to tell you? I *need* the money! So open the door and sign these papers. . . . Lawrence?"

Robert breaks into one of Grampa's long coughing fits. Then he says, "I'm not signing anything. You come back next Sunday, and then we'll talk. But leave me alone. And don't you bother Gwennie either. Now go away so I can take a nap."

After a pause Uncle Hank says, "And next Sunday you'll sign the papers? Is that a promise?"

"No promises. Send it all to my lawyer. I'm taking a nap."

Then Robert turns and shuffles noisily away from the door.

For ten seconds we both stand frozen, barely breathing, afraid to blink. Then we hear footsteps, hear the front door open and then slam shut. I dash to a parlor window and peek through the slats of the shutters. Uncle Hank is already stomping along the sidewalk toward Broadway, a file folder under one arm, hands stuffed in his coat pockets, shoulders stooped, head bobbing as he walks. I actually feel sorry for the man.

Robert says, "Pretty good, eh?"

I whip around and glare at him. "What, that you scared me to death? I can't *believe* you did that."

He shrugs. "It worked, didn't it? He would have

stood there banging on the door all afternoon. He might have even gone to get the police."

"And he still might, for all you know."

Robert shakes his head. "I don't think so. I predict he's off the radar screen for a solid week. And you can thank me anytime you want to."

I'm still glaring. "So what happens when he calls Kenneth Grant, or when he shows up next Sunday?"

He shrugs his shoulders. "I don't know. But I know that your Juilliard and Manhattan auditions will be over by Wednesday, and then you should be on your way to Boston for your tryout at New England Conservatory. If your grandfather's back, he can deal with Hank and the lawyer. And if he's not, then who knows? Not my job, and it's not your job either. We're just two kids trying to get into college, remember?"

Robert's exasperating, and he's got this superior attitude all of a sudden. And he's also right. Or almost right. Because even though I want my story to be that simple— that I'm just this kid trying to get into college—I know it's more complicated than that. It was always much more complicated, and I'm finally starting to figure that out. I mean, so many things had to happen just right, or I wouldn't even be here, wouldn't be doing any of this. So many others have been part of my story.

Still, it wasn't my mom and dad who boosted me onto this particular tightrope, and it wasn't Uncle Belden, or even Mr. Richards. Yes, they all had parts to play, and, yes, I owe a lot to each of them. But right now,

I owe the most to Grampa, who took me into his home, who built me a hideout in the basement. He's still holding one end of my tightrope, and right now, right when I want to see him, I can't. Because maybe he doesn't know how much I appreciate all his help. And that I still need it.

But Grampa's not here.

Then it occurs to me that it might also be nice to talk to Robert about this, about all of it, about my whole story.

But I'm too upset to talk, so I just say, "I'm going to practice."

"Good," Robert says. "That's the right thing to do."

As if I didn't already know that.

Because playing music is the one part of my story that's still absolutely my own.

chapter 11

NO STEAK

Walking down to the basement, I take deep breaths. I try to let all the stress dissolve. I try to put Robert and Uncle Hank and Grampa out of my thinking, push everything aside until there's nothing left except me and the music. Pyotr Melyanovich taught me that.

I can hear his thick Russian accent. "The music is not in your violin. The music is not in your bow or your technique. And the music is not in the notes on the page. A hundred years of practicing will not help one bit unless we have the music in here. *This* is where we must find the music, inside our hearts."

Sometimes I know what he means, but today it's not working. And I can imagine the judges on Tuesday, frowning, whispering to each other, shaking their heads. Who *is* this girl? And why did we decide to give *her* an audition? Because I'm playing all the right notes, but I don't hear the music. I'm glad Pyotr has taught me the difference.

On this Sunday afternoon I keep playing the notes anyway, running through every piece. Because that's important too, to have each note of each score burned into my mind and my fingers. The physical part of the performance needs to feel as natural as pouring water from a pitcher.

Still, with just two days to go, I should be feeling actual music. It should feel real. The composer's ideas ought to be burning the paint off my practice room walls. The emotions should be vaporizing the muscles and the violin and the fingers and the bow, until there's nothing left but pure thought. Because that's what a true performance is, and nothing less will do.

And as I begin the *correnta* section of Bach's Partita number 1 in B Minor, I remember last night, playing for Robert in the dark. That was real music. And our trumpet-fiddle duet? That was music *and* poetry *and* life *and* everything else. Everything else that matters.

And as I sweep into the stately opening of the *sarabande* section, my mind jumps to Robert's question, about playing a fiddle tune for my teacher, about trying to close the gap between West Virginia and Lincoln Center.

So for a few measures, I pretend I'm Alison Krauss, and I introduce Bach to the Soggy Bottom Boys. But it's the wrong time for experimenting, so I toss my fiddle back into the hills and keep playing violin. Which is all the challenge I need at the moment.

Playing at performance level is exhausting. It's a real workout—mostly for the mind, but the body feels it too. I keep practicing until my fingertips hurt and my neck and arms are aching. And then I stop, because that's important too—knowing when to rest.

When I walk back upstairs, Robert has the score of the Haydn concerto spread across the dining table, and he's tapping out the notes on the buttons of his trumpet. I'm not mad at him anymore.

He looks up and says, "How'd it go?"

"Not great. But I ran through everything from memory. So that's good. Want some food before you practice?"

He nods. "I'm starved. Got anything like a burger? I could walk over to that market on Broadway and get something to cook." I get the feeling Robert looks for excuses for walking around New York, and I don't blame him. It's an amazing place. But he could wander off for an hour, and I'm too hungry.

I shake my head. "How about a steak? We've got some downstairs in the freezer."

I start to turn back toward the stairs, and he says, "I'll go get it. You look beat."

He's trying to be nice, so I let him. I smile and say, "Thanks. The freezer's in the utility room, past the door that goes down to the basement. You can't miss it."

Then I go to the oven and turn on the broiler.

A minute or so later I'm putting water into a pot to

start cooking some green beans when Robert comes back into the kitchen. His hands are empty, and he looks a little confused.

"The steaks are wrapped in white paper. Didn't you see them?"

He shakes his head. "You better go down and look for yourself."

I'm thinking it's odd he couldn't find the steaks, but mostly I'm focused on getting dinner ready, because I'm starved.

So I walk across the parlor and then down the stairs to the ground floor, and I can hear Robert following behind me.

I go past my bedroom door, along the hallway, and into the utility room. And I open the lid of the big freezer, because I know there has to be a steak or a roast we can cook up for supper.

And in the dim light I see my grandfather. Grampa's in the freezer.

I don't scream, partly because Robert is standing so close behind me. But I gasp, and then I push out a breath, and it turns into a small white cloud that hangs in the frozen air.

I just stare at Grampa's face.

And I'm numb until a twinge in my chest makes me think back to when I was little, back in West Virginia. Because I've been to plenty of funerals, and sometimes they don't close the lid on the coffin.

When you go to a funeral home, you know that you

might see a body there, so you're sort of ready for it. And I remember when we drove for a Sunday afternoon visit with Mama's aunt Irene, and we all knew she hadn't been well, and I knew that we might get there too late, and Aunt Irene would be gone. Except for her body.

It's a big freezer, an old Kelvinator. When it's late at night and the compressor turns on, I can hear it from my bedroom.

I don't want steak anymore, so I close the lid. Gently.

chapter 12

SUPECTS

I think you're going into shock."

That's what Robert says. But I don't feel like I'm in shock. I don't even know what that is, going into shock. I feel confused, that's all. Like I ought to be crying. Like I ought to be horrified, screaming and moaning, sitting with my legs pulled up against my chest, rocking back and forth.

But I'm not doing any of that.

I'm just standing in front of the big freezer, and there's fog all around me. I'm just confused. I don't understand why Grampa's in the freezer, that's all. I don't understand.

Robert takes my hand, and he leads me upstairs to the parlor. He puts me on the couch, and he pulls a chair over and sits facing me.

He says, "I'm sorry. I'm sorry I did that. I'm sorry I made you walk down there and look. I don't know why I thought you should see him for yourself. But what was I going to do? Walk up here and say, Hey, I think the man in the freezer is your grandfather? I couldn't do it, Gwen. But I probably should have. So I'm sorry. Really."

There's a big blue pillow next to me on the couch, and I pull it onto my lap, and then hug it with both arms. I look at Robert's face, and he's so pale, I can see little freckles on his nose. He's the one who looks like he's going into shock. He's got his hands pressed between his knees, and I notice he's wearing the new running shoes. From our trip to the store today. Which seems like years ago.

Time isn't working anymore.

I hear myself say something. "We have to call the police." My voice sounds like it's out there, somewhere far away. I say it again. "We have to call the police."

Robert nods. "Right. Yes. We do. Do you . . . do you think your uncle did it? Put him in there?"

I whimper and groan and wail all at the same time. Because the *how* question had not hit me, not until this moment. And the question hurts. How did this happen?

And I'm seeing my dad's face when he learns about his father. About how Grampa was found.

But I see why Robert had to ask the *how* question. Because this is not an accident, that my grampa's in the freezer. Who could do that? And why? Could Uncle Hank do that? Could anyone?

How?

An aged man is but a paltry thing,
A tattered coat upon a stick . . .

It's from "Sailing to Byzantium." Yeats is no comfort.

I'm still in the fog, and all I can think to say is, I'm so sorry, Grampa, I'm so sorry.

Grampa's face. I want to see him smile. I want to hear him laugh when that guy on *Wheel of Fortune* makes a bad pun. It's not going to happen.

And the reality of the situation around me begins to take shape in my mind. Because I can see a murder investigation, right off a true-crime TV show. It's coming. I'm seeing technicians dusting for fingerprints. I'm seeing men and women with rubber gloves and little flashlights poking into every corner of the house, every corner of Grampa's life. Every corner of my life too.

And my story, that simple story of a girl trying to get into music school, my story feels like it's been swallowed up whole, the way an owl eats a mouse.

Then it's like this huge gust of wind pushes through my mind and all the fog is gone. Everything snaps sharp and clear.

It's my voice again, closer now. "You have to leave, Robert. Right now. Before I call the police. You need to get back to your hotel. You were never here. This is a mess. A huge mess. And it's got nothing to do with you. Unless you stay. So you've got to go. Right now, okay? And I'll go around and wipe off all your fingerprints. No one will know you were here. So go, okay?"

"I can't do that."

The look on Robert's face. Very sweet. And protective.

I say, "But you *have* to go. This is going to ruin every-thing for me, but it's not your problem. It's my grampa, and it's my problem. So go. But first help me go through the house and clean up."

He shakes his head. "I really can't leave—I mean, think about it. I'm a witness here. Because you're a sus-pect too. I can't leave. They'd find out I was here any-way. Think how many people on this block have seen me go in and out with you. And if you wiped my finger-prints off the freezer, you might wipe away something the police will need. We have to tell them everything, tell it exactly the way it happened. Even the part about me faking the voice to your uncle Hank. I might get in some trouble for that, but if I walk away, *that's* a real crime. This is serious. And I'm probably a suspect too."

I'm hearing what Robert is saying, but I'm stuck back near the beginning. That one thing he said: *Because you're a suspect too.*

Me, a suspect. In the mysterious death of my own grandfather. A suspect.

So I go into the study, and I pick up the phone. But then I hang up.

Robert's watching me. "What're you doing?"

I don't want to explain myself. I pull my cell phone from the pocket of my jeans, and I punch the menu but-ton until I find the call log, and then I scroll until I see a number I don't recognize. I push Dial, and after five rings it goes to voice mail: "This is Kenneth Grant. Please leave a message."

After the beep I say, "Mr. Grant? This is Gwendolyn Page, Lawrence Page's granddaughter. I just found my grampa. He's . . . dead. He's in the freezer, here at his house. In the utility room. And I have to call 911. And I wanted to ask you what else I should do. Because you said I should call if I needed any help. And I . . . I need help."

Then I push the End button, because that's all there is to say.

Robert's nodding. "That was a good idea."

I sit in the big desk chair. It's so still, so quiet in this house. I love that silence. I wish it could stay like this, so calm. I need to think. I want to run down to my practice room and shut myself in. I need to play my violin, right now. I need to play Bach, to feel his calm and the perfect order of his ideas.

"Gwen?"

It's Robert. I shut my eyes and shake my head. "Shhh."

"Gwen—you have to call the police. Now."

I open my eyes. I pick up the handset from the desk phone and the sharp dial tone fills the study. I push 9, and then 1, and then I stop. Still holding the phone, I swivel to face Robert.

"Who says we have to call the police right away? Why not wait, wait until Mr. Grant calls back? Or even wait until tomorrow? Or Tuesday? I mean, it's horrible and everything, about Grampa, but the second we call the police, then everything goes completely out of control. And Grampa wanted me to keep working, to follow through on my auditions. He wanted me to."

But even as those words come out, I know I'm being irrational. And disgustingly selfish. And I already wish I hadn't said it.

Robert's shaking his head. "Gwen—no. You have to call now. Someone is *dead*. Downstairs. You have to call the police right now. Do it."

I have to call now. Of course I do. If I try to delay the chaos, it'll be that much worse when it hits.

So I punch in the number.

"911—what is your location?"

A woman's voice, and I tell her.

"Tell me your emergency."

"I . . . I just found my grandfather. He's dead."

"Your name?"

"Gwendolyn Page."

"Did this just happen? Does he need a paramedic?"

"No. He's . . . he's in a freezer."

"Please repeat that."

"He's in a big freezer. He's . . . dead."

"Are you in danger?"

"No. There's no danger."

"All right. You stay where you are. And don't touch anything. Officers are on the way."

That was the end of call number two.

By the time I'm done with the 911 operator, I'm sobbing. It's because I keep having to say "he's dead." And it's hitting me again, harder. My grampa is gone. And

I'm not going to get to talk to him again. No more bed-time snacks, no more orders, no more salutes. The only picture I can see of Grampa right now is what I just saw, downstairs. It's not fair.

And now the tears, hot and angry. Our little terrier, who got run over by the mail truck, and my cat Gracie, who died right in my arms. And Aunt Irene, who passed on that Christmas—I'm crying for all of them, for everyone and everything I have ever loved. And I'm crying like I did that night I was ten, sitting alone out on the front porch, when I knew for the first time that Daddy and Mama wouldn't live forever. And now my grampa.

After a few minutes Robert leans over and puts an arm around me. I feel my shoulders shaking. I'm glad he didn't leave.

I force myself to stop crying, force myself to be quiet. Because I am the brave one. I am the brave one.

And that's good, because I have to make another call.

I click to the speed-dial list in my cell phone and punch the top number.

"Hello?"

That voice sounds so good to me. "Mama?"

"Well, hi, Gwennie. I knew it would be you calling. How are you, sweetheart? Have you been havin' a nice Sunday?"

"Mama, I have to talk to Daddy." My voice sounds funny, and my mom knows it.

"Are you all right, dear? Is something wrong?"

"I'm fine, Mama, but . . . Grampa died. And I need to tell Daddy."

"Oh, my! . . . All right, dear. Here's your father."

My dad's a big man, built like Uncle Hank. I love hearing his deep voice.

"Hey, it's my big city girl. How're you doing up there?"

"Daddy? It's Grampa. He's . . . passed on. I'm sorry to be the one who has to tell you."

My dad is quiet, and I can picture him as he gets all still and serious. And I remember all the stories Daddy told me about him and Grampa, about hunting and fishing together. And how Grampa almost cried the day Daddy left for Vietnam.

But my dad is also the brave one. He clears his throat and says, "Was it . . . there at home? It wasn't an accident or anything, was it?"

"No, not an accident, I don't think. But it's . . . unusual, Daddy. Because Grampa's in the big freezer, the one in the utility room. And I don't know . . . how it happened. So it's . . . unusual. I had to call the police. I'm sorry to have to tell you this."

A second of silence, then, "Did you say in the freezer? You sure about that?"

"You can't make a mistake about something like this, Daddy."

I hear the intercom buzzer at the front door.

My dad says, "Well, I'm coming up there tonight if I can—tomorrow, for sure. Are you all right until then? Do you want me to call Uncle Hank for you?"

"No, don't do that, Daddy. I have a friend here who's helping me. And I called Grampa's lawyer, too. So I'm okay. I've got to go now, Daddy. The police are here. I love you."

"I love you, too, Gwennie. And I'll be there right away. And I'll call. Here's your mama again."

"Gwennie? Now don't you be afraid. Everything'll work out. You just tell everybody the truth, and then trust it all to God, you hear? You're bein' watched over, same as always."

"I know, Mama. Thank you. I have to go now. I'll call back in a bit. I love you."

"I love you too, sweetheart."

I put the cell phone in my pocket, and the intercom buzzes again. And Robert and I walk out to open the door for the police.

Except when I open the door, it's not the police.

chapter 13

TOO MUCH

efore I can react, Uncle Hank pushes past me into the front hall, brushes Robert aside and walks through the open parlor door.

"Lawrence?"

I'm inside now, and Uncle Hank's in the study.

"Robert! In here!" He follows me at a dead run into Grampa's bedroom, and I slam the door and lock it.

"Lawrence!" His big fist shakes the door in its frame. "Are you in there? Tell Gwennie to open the door. I need to talk to you, right now."

Robert and I have our shoulders against the door. And I can see Robert beginning to make his old man face, and he takes a breath: He's about to start talking like Grampa again.

So I poke him in the side, and I shout through the door. "Just go away. This isn't a good time. So just leave." Because in the back of my mind I guess I think I can keep Uncle Hank out of all this for another day or so. There's already too much to deal with.

Uncle Hank bangs the door again. "I want to see him. And who's that kid in there with you? That your boyfriend or something? What's going on around here, Gwennie? Open this door, or I'm going to give it a good kick and come in anyway."

"Hold it, mister! Police! Hands on the wall, and don't turn around!"

"What the—? Oh, great! Nice going, Gwennie. You had to go and be stupid and call the police."

I open the bedroom door, and there are two officers, both men, one with a hand on his pistol. The second officer has his left hand against Uncle Hank's back, and he's patting around with the other to check for weapons.

It takes all my courage to speak. "I'm Gwendolyn Page. I'm the one who called 911."

The officer finishes with Uncle Hank and says, "What's the yelling about?" And to me he says, "You know this man?"

I nod. "He's my uncle."

Still talking to me, he says, "And you live here?"

I nod. "With my grampa. It's his house."

Uncle Hank snarls, "And it's my house too."

The second officer says to Hank, "Just keep it quiet unless someone asks you a question, okay?" Then to me he says, "And you're the one reported the dead body, right? You want to show me now?"

I nod at the officer, but I'm watching my uncle's face. The anger drains away. Seconds later I'm looking at a different man, more like a boy. Somebody's little brother. "Body?" he says. "What body?"

Hank turns from the officer and locks eyes with me. "Gwennie? Is it . . . it's Lawrence?"

My eyes fill with tears, and I nod.

The crumpled face, the pain in his eyes. And I cross Uncle Hank off the list of suspects. Because I believe his sadness and shock, believe it completely.

The officer nods at Robert and asks me, "Who's he?"

"A friend of mine. He found it first . . . the body."

Uncle Hank moves to the couch and slumps into the cushions, face in his hands.

"Okay, then," the officer says. "Why don't you two lead the way."

The next ninety minutes feel like a dream. After Robert and I show the policeman the freezer, he calls for an evidence team. Fingerprint dusting, dozens of photographs, a medical examiner from the coroner's office, a body bag, an ambulance.

Robert and Uncle Hank each spend about fifteen minutes in the study giving their statements to the man in charge, Detective Keenan. Jason the tenant shows up, and he gets questioned too. And a technician takes fingerprint samples from all of us, "for the process of suspect elimination," he says.

By the time it's my turn to give a statement, Kenneth

Grant arrives, and he comes into the study with me. I start with how I came home from my violin lesson on Thursday. I play Grampa's message, and after it rewinds, the detective takes the whole answering machine and puts it into a plastic evidence bag. I tell the entire story, right up to calling Mr. Grant and the police and my parents, and then Uncle Hank pushing his way into the parlor.

When I'm done, Mr. Grant says, "Detective Keenan, I've got some information that may or may not be important. Thursday was the last day my client was seen alive, and it was also the day he left a message on my office voice mail. He told me that an envelope was on its way to me, and he asked me not to open this envelope except in the event of his death. He also asked me to call on Friday and check to see if his granddaughter was all right, which I did."

"Where is it, this envelope?" It's clear the detective doesn't care much for lawyers.

"In a safe at my office. I haven't opened it. It's registered mail."

"I'll send an officer to get it."

The lawyer pauses. "Actually, since I am the addressee, the contents are privileged client information. And there's nothing that automatically links this envelope to your case." The detective stiffens, and Mr. Grant quickly adds, "But I want to cooperate in every way, so I'll be happy to bring the envelope wherever you'd like me to, and I'll open it in your presence. Then we can determine together if any of the contents are relevant."

The detective's not completely happy, but he says, "Three P.M. tomorrow at the Twenty-fourth Precinct house—100th Street between Amsterdam and Columbus. We'll have a probable cause of death by then." Turning to me, the officer says, "I want you to be there, and your boyfriend too. And neither of you leaves the city until this is settled."

"Oh . . . he's not my boyfriend."

"Just tell him not to go anywhere, okay?"

As quickly as the craziness began, it ends. The patrolmen, the technicians, the detective, Mr. Grant, Jason from the third floor—everyone just leaves. Uncle Hank too. He trudges away to find a cab, looking ten years older. In a matter of five minutes they're gone, and it's Robert and me sitting by ourselves in the parlor.

It feels like a long time before either of us talks. Then Robert says, "I hate to mention it, but I'm still really hungry. You?"

I nod. I hate to admit it too. It seems disrespectful to eat, to do something so normal right here in Grampa's house, right where he'll never be again.

Then, for the first time, I understand why there's always food after a funeral, at least in my family. Food and eating are all about life, about keeping up the strength to go on. And Grampa would want that. He truly would.

I feel drained, but I get to my feet and move toward the kitchen. "How about a ham and cheddar omelette? Maybe with some mushrooms?"

Robert smiles. "That'd be great."

I turn the corner and bend down to get the frying pan from the cabinet below the cooktop. And I hear, "If you don't mind, I'd like an omelette as well. And some toast with jam. Sounds quite delicious."

It's an almost perfect British accent, and I know Robert means well, trying to lighten things up. But I'm not in the mood. So I say, "Please, no joking, not now."

"Awfully sorry—though I must say that merely requesting sustenance can hardly be construed as humour."

The idiot's still being British, so I put my head around the corner. "I'm serious, Robert, not now."

Then I see his face. It's chalky white, and Robert's eyes are wide, locked, staring at the space in front of the fireplace. So I look there too.

And there it is. Just like at the Nike store.

It's the shadow man.

chapter 14

UNINVITED

ear is an excellent cure for fatigue. It even dulls
my grief. I'm instantly alert, looking at the vague,
wavy shadow of an invisible person, a man,
standing in the parlor.

And then I remember what Robert said about being
out in public: No clothes. There's a naked man standing
twenty feet away from me. A shiver grabes my spine
and shoots all the way to my toes. I know I have legs and
arms, but I can't seem to move them. I'm paralyzed.

Robert's not much better. At least he can talk. And
he can think too, because he begins looking wildly
around the room, and he says, "What's going on? Who's
that talking?" He's pretending he doesn't know what's
happening. And I don't really understand why.

The man chuckles. "Nice try, my good fellow. But
you see, I heard you talking to the young lady on the
subway this afternoon. It's Gwen, and I assume that's
short for Gwendolyn, right? You were telling Gwen-

dolyn about your experiences two years ago. So please, don't pretend to be confused."

Robert adjusts instantly. His face is still pale, but in a conversational tone, he says, "How come you followed us?"

"Curiosity, at first. I could tell you saw me. Which is nothing new. A person in my condition becomes sensitized to being noticed. This is at best a limited form of invisibility, and people are always catching glimpses of me."

"And how about dogs?" says Robert, and I can tell he's pulled that question from his own experience, his own time in the same condition. And it strikes me that my two guests, one invited and the other not, have a link, a strange bond that I can only imagine. But I'm learning fast.

The man laughs, and even his laughter has a British tone to it. "I have had to nearly throw myself in front of speeding taxicabs in order to avoid the teeth and claws of the city's canine residents. I have never seen so many ill-mannered four-footed creatures in my life. And, frankly, the two-footed New Yorkers are not much better.

"But getting back to your question, Robert: I followed you because you not only saw something—me—but you reacted in a way no one ever has before. You seemed to know *what* you were seeing. And when you began to practically run away, I knew I'd best investigate. I managed to catch up just as you got to Columbus

Circle. I didn't get to hear everything you said to Gwendolyn on the train—too many people about, and I had to keep retreating so as not to be trampled. But I heard enough to know that you and I should talk.

"So why don't we all sit at the table together? I often cook for myself, and I often nibble at some of the finest restaurants and delicatessens in the world. But a simple meal, cooked to order, is a luxury I've been craving for almost three years. Gwendolyn, are you planning to step over here and knock me senseless with that skillet, or may I prevail upon you to continue with your previously announced dinner preparations?"

The direct address wakes me up. I look down, and I'm still holding the frying pan.

"No, I'll cook. Omelettes. I'm ready."

"Excellent."

And as I dig around for ingredients in the refrigerator, the man says, "So tell me about your experience, Robert. And please, leave nothing out. I'm certain I shall know if you try to hold anything back."

It's the tone of his voice. Something unpleasant, almost threatening. I'm cracking eggs into a bowl, and from my position at the stovetop, I can see Robert on the couch, facing the fireplace. He gets this wonderfully simple look on his face and says, "Why would I hold anything back? Besides, there's not that much to tell. I woke up one morning at my house in Chicago and I was invisible. And I was that way for almost a month. I stayed at home with my parents, and we kept it a secret.

And then one morning I woke up, and I was back. I had some fun, and I missed a lot of school. And I learned more about what I want in life. Because that time changed the way I look at myself. And other people. But that's about it."

So Robert's holding back, telling as little as possible. I don't blame him.

The man makes a clucking sound, and I can imagine him shaking his head. "No, no, no—that's far too simplified. I want details, young man, all the details. After a month in the shadow world, you went to bed invisible one night, and then you woke up normal again? Is that what you're saying?"

Robert nods his head. "That's what happened. Was it different for you? I mean, like, at the start? And, who are you?"

"Call me William, please. I was employed as a rather undistinguished assistant professor of English literature at a university some distance north of here. Three winters ago I awoke at four in the morning needing a drink of water, and I went to the kitchen in my flat and reached for a glass, and—no hand. No hand, no arm, nothing visible beneath my pyjamas. I had been divorced for two years, living on my own, writing literary criticism when not teaching. So, unlike you, I faced my predicament alone. And that night my former life came to an abrupt end. I simply disappeared, which I must say I found quite invigorating. Rather like being reborn. No debts, no more whining from my ex-wife, no more alimony or child-support payments—quite delightful." He chuckles and then adds, "I even got to settle a few old scores at the university before I left."

Warning bells go off in my head, because I've never liked the kind of person who holds a grudge. And again, I feel a dark undercurrent—something almost cruel. Something dangerous.

Robert has to be feeling the way I do, but he's nodding, playing along. He says, "But now you want to get back to normal again."

The man pauses, considering Robert's statement. "I would at least like the option. I'd like to know how this happened. Which is why you, young man, are of such intense interest to me. You see, being in this state has enabled me to develop a way to make quite a lot of money. However, at some point it would be good to become my former self so I can spend that money in more conventional ways than I'm currently able to. It does one little good to be stinking rich if one cannot purchase a villa in a sunny climate and then live at that villa without alarming the local population. A person who looks like me cannot speed about in an expensive motorcar without being covered with clothes from head to toe, and of course, that takes all the fun out of owning a convertible. So I'm keenly interested in how you returned to ordinary life." He pauses, then adds, "And I think you are not telling me all you know about it."

With a look of confused innocence, Robert says, "There's nothing more to tell. It's not like I planned for it to happen, and I didn't plan for it to stop, either. It happened, and then it stopped."

Robert may be the best actor I know. And now I understand exactly why he's holding back like this. The goal is to say good-bye to this man as soon as possible. But what if he decides he wants to stick around? What happens then?

I've got the first omelette almost ready, so I put two pieces of bread in the toaster. "William, do you want some orange juice with your omelette? Or milk? Or coffee? And what do you want on the toast? There's orange marmalade, strawberry preserves, and grape jelly." It's strange to be talking to someone I can't see, because the man isn't in front of the mantel anymore, and it's exactly like Robert told me: If you're in that state, no one can see you unless you're right up against another background.

And when the man answers, I jump, because William's just opposite me, right on the other side of the island where I'm cooking. Close enough to reach across the stovetop and touch me. Another shiver.

"Orange juice will be perfect, and strawberry preserves. No coffee, thanks. And you do not have to shout in my direction, Gwendolyn. I am presently invisible, but my hearing is unimpaired."

And the smile in the man's voice tells me that he enjoyed seeing me jump.

By the time the toaster pops, I've got three places set at the table, and then I serve the first meal. "All ready."

I've moved my daffodils, and I place William's food on the table so he's facing me as I cook the second omelette. I don't want to miss anything. Robert can be matter-of-fact about this, but it's all new to me, and I want to see—or not see—the whole magic act. And then I want this man to leave.

I have to admit that mealtime is quite a show. The knife floats, slices off a tab of butter, and then spreads it onto the toast. The salt and pepper rise into the air and take turns shaking above the omelette. The juice glass goes up, tips, and the liquid seems to spill into midair and disappear. The fork is in almost constant motion, cutting, spearing, ferrying back and forth between plate and mouth.

And I'm overcooking the second omelette.

Robert's at the table now, and between mouthfuls the man keeps talking. I wish he'd talk with his mouth open so I could see the food floating there before he swallows. But he has proper English table manners.

"As I followed you here, I was hoping to walk indoors behind you so we'd have a quiet moment to begin our conversation. And then I saw that large man, Henry Carlton Page, as I recall the name, who began pounding on the door. You two made such a dash that I couldn't slip into the house with you, and I had to stay outside for most of the afternoon. I didn't think it wise to ring the bell."

Robert says, "Weren't you freezing?"

"It was not pleasant, but unless it's bitterly cold, I

have trained myself to ignore bodily discomfort. Then the police arrived and opened all the doors, and I've been admiring your home ever since, Gwendolyn. And I must say, this is quite a ripping little drama you've got going here. After my initial tour of the premises, I took up residency in the library, since that seemed to be the police command center. And I listened to all of the statements taken by that dreadful chief inspector. And I shall be quite interested to see what he makes of the case. And, of course, Gwendolyn, I am truly sorry about the loss of your grandfather. He has a kindly face. The police were very respectful of him—which is more than they've ever been to me. It was fascinating to watch them do their work. Real life is far more interesting than television, don't you think?"

After a sip of orange juice, the glass hangs in midair, and he says, "I just *adore* nosing about in other people's business, don't you? In fact, I often think I should start my own private detective agency. Because sometimes I'll just choose a person who's walking down the street, someone who looks interesting to me, and I'll follow along for days and days—home, office, gym, restaurants, even business trips, and those quiet evenings with friends and family. It's fascinating to learn so much about another human being, all those little secrets. Of course, I snoop mostly because it's amusing, just because I can. But I'm certain I would be paid handsomely for the information I could discover. But it's not a job for the faint of heart. I've had some rather close calls as an amateur. So it's probably just as well that I've found . . . other work."

Robert's omelette is served, and as I pour out the egg mixture to start cooking mine, I notice my hands are shaking. But I'm curious, and I say, "So, what is this other work?" It's a casual question, but right away I feel like I shouldn't have asked.

The juice glass descends. Then a napkin lifts slowly off the table, dabs the air, and returns to its place. And his voice says, "I'd rather not go into that. But I can tell you that it's an endeavour that has a kinship with the grand old English tradition of Robin Hood."

I flip my omelette. And even though the man scares me, I'm still curious. So I ask another question. "Do you just sleep in stores . . . like, anywhere it's warm?"

"Do you mean, am I a homeless person? No, I rent a comfortable flat north of Fourteenth Street, situated above what used to be a meat-cutting plant. It's a one floor walk-up, and I have my own door at street level with an electronic entry pad—which saves me the trouble of keeping track of a key. I come and go whenever I wish, and my neighbors do not seem to notice or care when my door opens and closes at odd hours. New York is a lot like London in that way, everyone basically minding his own business. I have groceries delivered to my entryway once a week. I did have a break-in last September, but the burglar took an unfortunate tumble down my stairs—I waited until he had a television in his arms. Poor lad thought no one was home. And as he lay at the bottom of the stairs with a broken ankle, sharp things like forks and pencils began to mysteriously float through the air and then suddenly jab into his arms and legs. Quite a lot of howling. The fellow finally managed to flee with relatively minor injuries, but I am certain that neither he nor any of his colleagues will ever be back. He had a *frightening* experience."

I'm having the same experience, right now. I flinch as the last of William's omelette disappears, followed by the final few bites of toast. And I can imagine the flexing of his jaw muscles as he chews, imagine him reaching up with a long fingernail to pick a scrap of food from his teeth. There's a smirky sneer on his face. I don't have to see it to know it's there. Maybe he was a decent person back in his former life, but not anymore, and I don't want him in my home, or in my life, or anywhere near me. Compared to this man, my uncle Hank is a teddy bear. Yes, Uncle Hank's been a bully. But William—if that's even his name—William is doing stuff that's really nasty, and he's doing it on purpose. And he's smirking because he knows he can get away with anything he wants to. And if I could, I'd push him out the door right now, this instant.

I'm at the table now, and I take a drink of orange juice. It tastes sour. Everything seems to have turned sour. Sour and surreal.

"Something wrong, Gwen?" There's a mock-caring tone in William's voice.

I shake my head and turn my attention to my plate, angry that I let my thoughts show on my face.

He goes on, his voice oozing sarcasm. "You look as if you're disturbed about something. Ahh, of course—your grandfather. Poor dear. How insensitive of me. And here I am, intruding on your grief, even making you cook for me. I should be ashamed of myself, I really should. I'm afraid I haven't made a very good first impression."

His chair scoots back from the table, and Robert gets to his feet as well.

"I must be going now. Robert, if you'll escort me to the door, that would be grand. And when I'm standing on the front steps, we shall shake hands like gentlemen, and that way you'll know for certain that I'm outside. And that way you'll both sleep better tonight—knowing that I'm actually gone. Or at least, actually . . . outside."

Again, the smirk. His voice has moved across the parlor and the hallway door opens. Robert follows, and then the street door opens. And watching from beside the table, I see Robert put out his hand, and there's a shake, and then Robert's inside again, fast, shutting both doors. "And put the bar in place," I say, but Robert's ahead of me, already fitting the bottom of the brace rod into its floor socket.

He walks back to the table and sits across from me. "That is one creepy guy."

I nod and then shiver. "He's awful. And I'm sorry I doubted what you told me earlier. But until it's right there, it's just too . . . unbelievable."

Because this afternoon on the subway when I dropped Robert's story into the same bucket with Belinda's alien adventures, I couldn't see how this invisibility stuff would ever affect my own little story.

And now William has changed that. My story has been picking up a lot of passengers recently. Too many.

I say it again. "So I'm sorry I doubted you."

Robert waves my apology aside. "But now what do I do?" he asks. "Because no way am I going to tell this guy how to reverse the process. He shouldn't have that information. He's a crook—you heard him. He's Robin Hood. That means he steals from rich people, which has to be why he likes it here in New York. Except I bet he doesn't give a cent to the poor—or anyone else. But I already figured that out."

I stare at Robert. "What do you mean? Figured what out?"

"It was in yesterday's newspaper. There's a big story in the *Times* about more than a dozen unsolved robberies. Van Cleef and Arpels, Bulgari, Harry Winston— all the top jewelry stores in the city. A salesperson and a customer will be sitting across from each other, and the customer is looking at some rings or necklaces— things that cost two or three hundred thousand dollars each—and suddenly, one or two of the items is missing. Just missing. It's not the salesperson stealing, and it's not the rich customer. So guess who's taking the stuff? William reaches over, closes his hand around a nice chunk of jewelry, and it disappears. Then he walks out the door and probably makes a phone call to somebody who can sell it for him. And the same sort of shoplifting has been happening at all the big diamond wholesalers on Forty-seventh Street. Our new friend is a major thief. And the most recent store was Tiffany and Company— three robberies in the last two weeks. And do you know where Tiffany's is? Right at Fifty-seventh and Fifth Avenue. Which is just around the corner from Niketown. It has to be him."

I'm quiet a minute, trying to sort through everything. I can't, so I ask, "So what should we do? We have to do *something*, don't we? Shouldn't we tell the police?"

Robert shakes his head. "Because what happens if it becomes this huge news story—because it would—and suddenly everyone knows there's a way to make a person disappear? The FBI and the CIA would get on the case, I'm sure of that. And they'd figure it out. They would. Because the first thing that guy would do is tell them about me. And then my parents would be involved. And then Alicia and her parents. Because this process is dangerous technology, especially if it gets into the wrong hands. And it would all come out. It would all come out. . . ."

His thoughts trail off, and he looks tired and confused.

I look at my watch, and it's almost seven-thirty. It

feels more like three A.M. I'm beyond tired, beyond drained, beyond exhausted. I'd like to go to bed, or at least take a nap. Then I think about my bedroom.

I'm not a superstitious person, but I don't want to go downstairs to my bedroom. Downstairs is where Grampa was.

And while I'm wondering if Robert is bothered by stuff like that, he says, "Are you going to think I'm terrible if I tell you that I want to stop thinking about all this and go down to the basement and practice awhile?"

So that answers that. He's not only fine about going downstairs, he's going to walk right up to the yellow crime scene tape stretched across the back hall, take a right turn, walk down into the dim basement, and then play his trumpet.

I shake my head. "No, that's fine. You need to. I'm just going to stretch out here on the couch and try to calm down. It's a lot to deal with in one day."

"Yeah it is," he says. Then a very sweet smile. "And you've been incredible, really. And it's my turn to do the dishes, okay?"

Before I can say thanks, he comes over and he's giving me a hug. And it makes me feel like I'm eight years old, sitting in the pickup, snuggled between my mom and dad on that long drive we took to Memphis, just the three of us, safe and warm on a country road with the wipers slapping rain from the windshield. I could stay folded against him like this for hours.

And then suddenly we're both embarrassed. We separate, and I say, "Thanks. For doing the dishes."

"Sure. No problem. Happy to help out," and he picks up his trumpet and goes down the stairs.

I take the dark green fleece blanket off the back of Grampa's recliner. I sit on the couch and try to make the room stop spinning. And it does.

Then I lie down. I spread out the blanket and curl up, pulling it around my shoulders. My mind wants to review the day, spin back through every detail, sort and file and categorize and judge every event, every person, every moment. But I don't allow it. I do what my mom told me to when I called home. She said I could trust it all to God. She said I was being watched over. And I reach out, because that's all I want, to be watched over. And I'm almost at peace, and then I'm crying. Because of Grampa.

It's the blanket. It smells like his aftershave.

But I calm myself again, and I trust Grampa to God as well. Because, honestly, there's nothing else I can do.

And sometimes trust has to be enough.

chapter 15

REINFORCEMENTS

Cell phone. My ring.

Morning light is coming through the shutters, and I'm tangled in the green blanket on the couch, trying to get the phone out of my pocket.

"Hello?"

"Hello, sweetheart—how're you doin' there?"

"Hi, Daddy. I'm fine. Are you coming?"

"I'm already in Newark, be at Penn Station in about an hour. I wanted to call last night, but your mama said you'd be in bed early after such a hard day. How'd everything go, with the police and everything?"

"It was okay. After about two hours everybody left. Except for Robert. He's a friend from the music camp at Tanglewood last summer. He's in the city for auditions, same as me. And I didn't want to be alone. Uncle Hank was here for a while too. So he knows about Grampa. And Mama was right. I fell asleep on the couch around eight o'clock."

I tell Daddy about the meeting at the police station

in the afternoon, and then he has to go get on his train. "See you soon, Gwennie."

Grampa's bedroom door is shut, and I'm thinking Robert is still asleep. Daylight makes the house more cheerful, so I walk downstairs to my room.

After I shower and dress, I go back upstairs and there's a note from Robert.

Have to run errands. Be back about noon. Practice!
Robert

I know it's good advice, to practice. And before, no one would have needed to remind me. But I can't. Daddy's coming, and the place needs to be tidied up. Robert did load the dirty dishes into the dishwasher, but he cleans up the way my big brothers do. The kitchen and dining area are still a mess.

I start to open all the shutters, and then I remember William. For all I know, he's right outside, trying to see into the house. It's a bad feeling, and I leave the windows covered.

After I finish the dishes, I walk to the table, pick up the chair William sat on, and put it over in the corner. I don't want to use that chair again. It should probably be reupholstered. Or burnt.

Then I move the daffodils back to the center of the table, and they're still as bright and fresh as ever, *Tossing their heads in sprightly dance*. Thank you, Mr. Wordsworth.

Robert's back a few minutes before my dad arrives, and I'm glad, because I want my dad to meet him. But as the front buzzer sounds, Robert smiles at me and then disappears down the stairs with his trumpet.

"Hey, there she is!"

In the middle of my dad's bear hug, I remember how much I love my family, remember how much it means to have that love, always there. But even during this sweet moment in the doorway, at least half my mind is watching, on high alert, making sure there's not room for someone to slip past us into the house. The William thing is making me completely paranoid. Robert made me promise not to tell my dad or anyone else about that situation.

But there are plenty of other things to talk about, and we do, for almost an hour, and during that time neither of us says anything about Grampa. And as we talk, my dad does a good job of hiding how sad he is that his own dad is gone now. But I can still tell he's torn up about it. Because I know how I would feel.

When Robert comes back upstairs, right away my dad grabs his hand and says, "I want to thank you for taking care of my little girl last night. Means a lot to me."

Robert's sort of embarrassed, but he smiles back and says, "Sure, no problem. I mean, it's not like she wasn't doing great on her own. But I was glad to be here."

"So," Daddy says, "what d'you think's gonna happen at the meeting, at the police? Got any clues?"

It's hard to remember that my dad grew up in Queens. His accent sounds like pure West Virginia. Which I think is actually much nicer.

I shrug. "There's that letter Grampa sent to his lawyer. That's got to be important, don't you think?"

Robert nods his head. "Probably. Has to be important."

My dad says, "Well, we're all gonna know soon enough, I guess."

And he's right about that. We have time to eat some soup and sandwiches, and I get Daddy moved into Grampa's bedroom, with the sheets all changed and everything, and then it's time to walk to Broadway and hail a cab for the ride to the police station.

The Twenty-fourth Precinct station is on 100th Street next to a playground in the middle of the block. It's also close to an apartment complex called the Frederick Douglass Houses, more than a dozen buildings that fill most of the area between 100th and 104th streets. West Side High School is close too, and I get a quick look at the public school I'd attend if I actually lived around here. And if I didn't have a scholarship at Latham Academy. And if my family and my grampa hadn't helped me become a classical musician. So many ifs.

Mr. Grant is already inside the station waiting for us, and shortly after Detective Keenan takes us up a short flight of stairs to a conference room, Uncle Hank walks in. He and my dad have a quick hug. Both men are genuinely happy to see each other.

With a big smile, still holding my dad at arm's length, he says, "I don't think I've seen you since that summer before you went into the army."

My dad nods and says, "That was a real camping trip. Great memories, great memories."

And my perception of Uncle Hank shifts again. Because I can see how narrow a view I've had of the man. He really is someone's uncle, and someone else's little brother. I'm sorry it took something like this to make me figure that out.

I look around the room, and that's when I notice it's got one of those mirrored glass walls. And right away I get the feeling I'm being watched.

The detective takes charge, pointing at chairs for everyone, including a court stenographer, who moves to a corner facing us, sets up his portable keyboard, and then nods at the officer.

"Okay. First, let's see this letter you brought, Mr. Grant. And everyone, please speak clearly for the stenographer."

The lawyer reaches into his briefcase, pulls out a tan envelope, and passes it to the detective who's sitting across the table.

Detective Keenan says, "I am examining the postmark, which is Thursday of last week. This is a stamped and sealed registered mail envelope, and it has not been opened since received at the offices of Kenneth Grant, Attorney-at-Law."

He passes the envelope back to Mr. Grant. "Mr.

Grant will now open the envelope in clear view, and we'll determine together if any of the contents are relevant to the case at hand, that being the suspicious death of Lawrence Page, former resident of West 109th Street, New York City."

The lawyer tears open the envelope flap and pulls out three smaller sealed envelopes. Mr. Grant says, "There are three standard number-ten envelopes here, each sealed. One is addressed to me, Kenneth Grant. One is addressed to Henry Page, care of Kenneth Grant, and the third is addressed to Gwendolyn Page, also care of Kenneth Grant. And now I am opening the envelope addressed to me."

He does, and he takes out two handwritten pages, and reads them each silently. No one is talking, so the stenographer's fingers are still. Looking around the table, I'm the only one not trying to read the lawyer's face. Except Robert. He seems uncomfortable, and he's glancing around the conference room. Maybe the two-way mirror makes him jumpy. Then Robert notices I'm looking his way, and he flashes me a tense smile.

Clearing his throat, Mr. Grant passes the letter to the detective and says, "After you take a look at this, if there are no objections, I'll read each page aloud into the record. While this includes some personal business of the deceased, I believe it is relevant to these circumstances."

Detective Keenan scans the pages, says "I agree with that," and then hands the letter back.

Mr. Grant says, "For the record, I am reading from a

handwritten page, and am confident that the handwriting can be proven beyond all doubt to be that of my client, Lawrence Page." He adjusts his glasses and begins, first reading the date at the top of the page.

I am Lawrence Page, and I am writing this of my own free will, sitting alone in my own home.

Whoever's reading this knows that I'm gone now. I want anybody who's concerned, and I'm sure that's a number of people, to know one thing for certain: No one but me had any part in getting me into the freezer chest that's located on the ground floor of this home. This was my idea, and I put myself in there.

I'm sorry for the way it looks, and I'm sorry for the fright it must have given someone when I was found.

As I'm writing this, I'm at that point in my life where I know what's going to happen next. And I don't want anybody but me to feel responsible about making decisions—what to do, or what not to do for me—during my final days. So I have made my own decision.

Folks might disagree with what I've done, or the way I've done it, and I expect some will. But there it is. The people who know me and love me will understand, and they're the only ones I care about.

Lawrence Daniel Page

My dad wipes a tear from the corner of his eye, and Uncle Hank blows his nose into a handkerchief. And I'm crying too. I can hear Grampa's voice so clearly. I don't really understand why he did this. But I know that I'm one of the people who loves him. And Grampa says that I'll understand. So I will. I hope I will.

Detective Keenan pushes a box of tissues in my direction, and I take a few and say, "Thank you."

Mr. Grant then takes the second page from the envelope. "This," he says, "is not technically relevant to this proceeding, but I want to publish it into the record of this inquiry so there's no doubt that it came from the same envelope, and that it was written by the same person." And again he begins to read aloud.

I am Lawrence Page, and by my own hand I am revising my last will and testament. When and if the property on 109th Street is sold, from the part of the proceeds that belongs to my estate, I want enough money to be set aside to pay the entire cost of tuition, room, and board for the college and postgraduate studies of my granddaughter, Gwendolyn Page. If that property is not sold, then the necessary money should be taken from other available assets in my estate.

In addition, immediately upon my death, I want thirty-five thousand dollars taken from my personal funds and given to this same Gwendolyn Page for the purchase of a violin and a violin bow of her choosing.

I also want enough money to be provided from the funds of my estate so my granddaughter Gwendolyn Page can continue her musical studies here in New York without interruption until the end of this current school year.

These three provisions will be administered by my attorney, Kenneth Grant, as part of his duties as the executor of my estate.

Mr. Grant looks up and says, "And this codicil is signed by Lawrence Page and witnessed by Jason Di Renzo, of the same address as the deceased. It's dated on the last day that my client was seen alive."

Robert is smiling and nodding at me, and everyone looks pleased, even Uncle Hank. I'm all weepy again, but what the lawyer said doesn't surprise me. Here's my grampa, an hour or two before he dies, and he's thinking about someone else. It's beginning to fit.

Looking at the detective, Mr. Grant says, "Shall I open and read these other letters?"

The detective shakes his head. "I don't think it's necessary now."

So Mr. Grant reaches to his left and then his right, handing out the remaining letters, one to Uncle Hank and the other to me.

The policeman says, "We've got the preliminary

coroner's report, and as of this moment, this case is pretty much closed."

Mr. Grant raises his eyebrows. "So it's . . . suicide?"

And everyone else around the table winces at the word.

Detective Keenan says, "Actually, no. Mr. Page took a small oxygen bottle into the freezer with him, so he didn't suffocate. And he was all bundled up in his coat and cap and boots, so it wasn't the cold, either. And he'd put a piece of duct tape over the freezer latch, so he could have opened the lid and gotten out anytime he wanted to. The coroner is ninety-five percent certain that this man would have still passed on, no matter where he'd been at the time of his death. He chose a strange place to lie down, but it's accurate to say that he died in his sleep. According to the coroner, Lawrence Page died of natural causes."

Standing up abruptly, the detective walks to the door. "Sorry to rush everybody along, but I've got to ask you to leave now. We'll be in touch as needed."

And then the detective stands there, one hand on the doorknob, as the group files out of the room.

I'm the last one out, and I'm expecting the detective to follow me, but he doesn't. He slams the door shut on my heels, and then three other nonuniformed officers in the hallway line up at the door, knock once, and slip back into the conference room. One of the three men has a big video camera.

Before Daddy, Robert, and I are more than twenty

feet away, I hear shouting from the room, then the sound of furniture banging around.

I hesitate and look back, but Robert says, "C'mon, just keep going. That's got nothing to do with us."

But I stop and then Robert does too, and I look at him. Because it sounds like he's afraid.

Then from behind the closed door of the conference room, someone yells, "Get your *bloody* hands off of me!" It's a man's voice. And he has a British accent.

My heart stops, and I gasp. "Isn't that . . . ?"

But Robert shakes his head and makes a stern face at me. "Let's just go, okay?"

The others are already outside, so we go down the stairs and out of the police station, and then we hurry to catch up with my dad and Uncle Hank. Mr. Grant is already in a cab, and he turns and waves to me out the window. And I smile and wave back.

Then we're walking behind Uncle Hank and Daddy, and I start to say something to Robert, but he whispers, "Not now."

So as we cross Amsterdam Avenue and go downhill toward Broadway, I'm left with my own thoughts.

And I'm thinking that I don't believe what Robert said, that the commotion in the conference room has nothing to do with us.

Because I'm sure Robert's involved in this, right up to his dark brown eyebrows.

And that means I'm involved too. Even if I don't want to be.

chapter 16

COMEUPPANCE

My dad takes us all to a steakhouse for an early supper, so it's over an hour before I get to talk to Robert alone.

The meal feels awkward. There's only one thing on our minds, but none of us wants to talk about what Grampa did, or how the investigation turned out, even though it was as close to a happy ending as anyone could expect.

And those generous gifts to me are almost embarrassing. I feel like I've been picked as the favorite, Grampa's little pet. Even so, I can tell that the others are all happy for me, Uncle Hank included. Three times during the meal my eyes fill up with tears, thinking how sweet Grampa is to take such care of me.

Then Hank and Daddy start telling stories about growing up in Queens with Grampa and Grandmother, about trips to The Bronx Zoo and Coney Island and Jones Beach, and before long all four of us are laughing. And just when I'm starting to feel happy, my dad says,

"I called Veterans Affairs 'fore I left home, and since he's a decorated officer, they're gonna send us a color guard and a bugler, and they'll have a presentation flag too. He'd want you to have that, Hank." And the two men start talking about all the other arrangements for Grampa's funeral.

So I say, "If it's okay, Robert and I are going to walk back to Grampa's."

My dad says, "Sure, sweetheart, but I'd rather you took a cab."

I make a face. "Daddy, I'm a city kid, remember? Besides, it's not even dark yet."

He pushes a twenty-dollar bill into my hand. "Then here, take some money anyway and stop for a treat somewhere. You're pullin' out before dessert."

Robert thanks Daddy for the meal, and then we're outside. Before we're thirty feet from the restaurant, someone calls out, "Gwennie?"

I know that voice. It's Uncle Hank.

Robert says, "I'll wait here for you."

I walk back and when I stand in front of him, he talks fast, like he has to get it all out in one breath. "I feel bad, the way I acted, and about what happened. I wanted you to know that. Said some mean things too. Can't undo anything, but I wanted you to know. The fuel costs hit me, that's all. Couldn't even pay my drivers last week. It just . . . I just . . ."

This is hard for him. He's looking down into my face. "It's okay, Uncle Hank. And what happened, it wasn't your fault. I know Grampa didn't blame you. He even told me not to judge you. And I don't. I think everything's going to be all right, don't you?" Because that's what I hope.

He nods awkwardly, smiles a little. "Well, got to get back inside. See you soon, Gwennie."

"Bye, Uncle Hank."

I've been thinking of questions to ask Robert all during dinner, but we walk north on Broadway without talking. I've just been given a brand-new portrait of my uncle Hank, and I need to let the paint dry a little.

But after ten seconds, my curiosity won't be still. "So that was William, in the police station, right? And you went to the police and turned him in, right? Was that your errand this morning?"

Robert's got his hands stuffed into his jacket pockets. He slips me a sideways glance and half a smile. "I also made an important stop at that Italian bakery."

I ignore his attempt at humor, because this isn't funny, none of it. "But why did you think William would be at the police station?"

Robert shrugs. "Well, for starters he told us yesterday that he would be very interested to see how the case turned out. You remember that, right?"

I nod, and Robert says, "And he also bragged about what a hotshot snooper he is. But most of all, I was pretty sure William would come there to contact me again. I don't think I fooled him last night. At all. He *knows* that I know a lot more than I told him. And two years ago? I can remember how completely desperate *I* was to find out *anything*, to follow up *any* clue, even a tiny one, if it might mean I could get my life back again. And as far as William is concerned, *I* am a *huge* clue—a real break. He could have hung around this house and watched for me, but it's February, and it's cold out there. But he knew that I had to be at that police station at three P.M. today. So, was I sure he'd show up? No. But I'd have bet you my trumpet that he would. And he did."

"So . . . what did you tell the detective?"

"Ahh," Robert says. "That was the artistic part: To tell the truth, and nothing but the truth, but not quite the *whole* truth. I told Detective Keenan that there was this crazy guy who had slipped into your grampa's house yesterday during all the confusion, and that he was hiding in the study when everyone was giving their statements."

I nod. "So far, so true."

Robert ignores my commentary. "And then I told the detective that this crazy guy talked to us after everyone left, and that he said he was dying to know how the case would turn out. Also completely true. And then I told him that this man said he'd figured out a way to avoid the most sophisticated security systems, *and* that he'd been acting like a regular Robin Hood at some of the richest stores in Manhattan."

"So that's not *quite* the truth," I say.

"Close enough. And then I said, 'It's almost like this

guy thinks he's invisible or something. Which would make somebody into a pretty great thief.' "

"No! You said that?"

Robert grins. "Sure did. Because that's the big bait. Catching a broad-daylight robber would do a lot for a detective's career. And I also gave him William's juice glass, from the dinner dishes last night. So he could match fingerprints from the crime scenes. Because he had to leave fingerprints all over town. Invisible robbers can't wear gloves."

And standing there with my mouth open, it dawns on me just how far out of my league Robert is. The guy's a plotter. But I want to know the rest.

"So what'd he say—when you said that stuff about how he thinks he's invisible?"

"Well, the detective took this long pause, like a count-to-ten, because now he's not so sure about *me*. And he said, 'So you think he might try to hang around the meeting this afternoon, right in the police station?' And I say, 'This man seems to think he can get away with anything.' Also true, and also great bait for a detective. Then this was the crowning touch. I said, 'If he's so good at hiding himself, I think an infrared camera would probably make him show up plain as day.' "

"Robert!" I stop short on the sidewalk, and he faces me, beaming.

"And that's what they did. They lit up their camera, and they tracked his body heat right there in the room after we left. And it was four guys to one, so I'm thinking William the invisible creep is in jail. Right now."

I reach into my shoulder bag and pull out my cell phone. "Call him."

Robert looks at me like I'm insane.

"I mean Detective Keenan. Call him right now. I want to know, to really know that that man isn't walking around my neighborhood tonight. Because if he's still on the loose, and he wants to find you, he's going to come to Grampa's house again. And I don't want that to happen. Or if it might happen, then I want to be prepared. So call, okay? For me."

Robert takes the phone and calls 411 to get the nonemergency number of the Twenty-fourth Precinct.

"Hello? Could I talk with Detective Keenan? It's Robert Phillips calling."

Robert nods to me and whispers, "He's there."

"Detective? This is Robert. We talked about that crazy guy, remember? I just wanted to know if you got him. . . . Oh, that's too bad."

Robert shoots me a glance, and I gasp and grab his arm. He pulls loose and keeps talking.

"But I really called because I remembered something else he told me yesterday. He said he had an apartment north of Fourteenth Street, a first floor walk-up above an old meat-packing plant. . . . Right, with an electronic keypad instead of a lock. . . . Right. So I thought you should know about that. . . . Well, anyway, good luck." And Robert hangs up.

I'm frantic, and my voice has gone up an octave. "They didn't *get* him? Robert, that's really bad. It's terrible. Because he's not stupid, and he knows the police were looking out for him, and . . . and nobody could have told them but you. Or me. So now . . . now he *knows* that one of *us* tried to turn him in. And . . . and he'll try to do something, he'll—"

Robert waves his hands at me. "Hold it, hold it, hold it—calm down. The detective was lying to me. I'm sure they got him. No doubt at all. So just relax."

I'm stunned. "*Lying*? What do you mean? He's a *policeman*. Why would he lie? Police don't do that."

"Right," says Robert, "*unless* it's in the interest of public safety. If the police have a photo of a dangerous suspect, but the suspect doesn't know that, do they go on TV and say, 'We have no information at this time'? Yes they do, because that *lie* makes the suspect think he can walk around freely, and then the police can spot him and arrest him.

"Do you think that detective, who's got an invisible man in his custody, is going to tell people about it— even me? No way. And about the rest of it, whether William tells him about me being invisible and all that? I don't know what's going to come of that. But for now, I think the police are going to keep a tight lid on this, or maybe they'll make William an offer he can't refuse, make him go to work for them. Who knows? Anyway, I'm sure it was right to get him off the streets. So we've done our civic duty, and we'll have to see how all the rest of it works out. Because that's not our job. So. Where's the ice cream in this city?"

How Robert can think about ice cream right now is beyond my understanding. Of course, I've been on such an emotional seesaw today that everything is beyond my understanding.

But Robert turns on his ice cream radar, which guides us across 105th Street, where we find a sweets shop that's actually selling waffle cones in February, and he orders for both of us, two massive cones with three scoops each, whipped cream, nuts, sprinkles, the works. Then, by carefully decorating his nose with an assortment of toppings, Robert finally gets me to smile.

Even though I'm having a little fun, and even though I'm grateful for the good things that have happened today, I'm still uneasy about the William situation, and always, always, I feel this sadness that won't go away. Because I can't stop thinking about my grampa and that big freezer. About what he did.

And the selfish part of me is still wishing that all the complications would vanish. Because I want to get my story back. *My* story. I just want to be a musician, and suddenly, I know why.

It's because I've been imagining that it's going to be easy. It's because I think I'll be able to lose myself in great sweeps of harmony, and the all-knowing, infallible conductor will always lead the way. And me? I imagine myself gliding seamlessly from one movement to the next, with hardly a rustle as I turn the pages of the score.

Because I want things to work out the way they do when Bach is in charge. Or Paganini. Or Jane Austen. Or even Yeats. Because I'm desperate for a nice, tidy ending, maybe with a pleasant rhyme or two, or that wonderful last burst of symphonic harmony that makes me want to shout "yes!"

But it's not happening that way.

chapter 17

GIFTS

It's Monday night, and Robert tells me again that I should practice, but I say, "No, it's all right. You go first tonight." And like a gentleman, he goes down to the rehearsal room and leaves me alone.

With Daddy upstairs watching TV, I hide out in my room. I've talked to my mom for half an hour, said hi to both my sisters, and I've talked to both my big brothers. Plus I've had a call from Uncle Belden, and while we were talking, I could hear a West Virginia catbird singing, and I pictured its little throat moving, pictured it sitting in a tree out in front of his crooked front porch. And as he said good-bye, Uncle Belden wished me well on my auditions.

My auditions.

My first audition is at eleven tomorrow morning, but I don't care anymore. I don't want to go. There's a line in a Yeats poem that comes winging up out of my memory, and it slaps me hard:

Things fall apart; the center cannot hold;

And it hurts to feel this way. I'm so used to being Little Miss Organized and Little Miss Punctuality, and I've been a perfectionist for so long that I can't remember any other way to be. I didn't even get to my lesson this afternoon, and I missed my only practice session with the grad student who's doing the piano accompaniment on the Sibelius during my audition. It's like I don't know myself anymore.

I keep thinking about the questions Robert asked me this afternoon, after we'd had our ice cream. He said, "You know, I don't believe that, what your grampa said in his letter. He said, 'I'm at that point in my life where I know what's going to happen next.' And I don't think anybody can know that, do you? I mean, when he climbed into that freezer, like what was he thinking? Because you never know what's going to happen next, not really. You just have to take your best shot and keep hoping things'll work out. Right? Because no matter what the coroner says, I don't really think your grampa died of natural causes. Do you? I hate to say it, but it seems to me like he was kind of bailing out. And didn't he sort of create more problems than he solved? What do you think?"

The worst part is that I just kept shrugging my shoulders. I couldn't answer any of Robert's questions. I still can't. I wanted to say, "Well, if Grampa hadn't done what he did, I probably wouldn't have met you. And that would have been too bad." But I couldn't say that.

It's dark now, and I turn off the lights in my room so the place matches my mood. And I lie across my bed and stare up into nothing, and I think back just five days ago.

Last Wednesday night Grampa was sitting upstairs watching CNN. I'd had a good lesson with Pyotr Melyanovich, and I was down in the practice room making Sibelius smile. My first audition was still almost a week away, but I was going to be ready. I was building up my confidence. I was almost at the peak of my preparation, and soon I would march across the plaza at Lincoln Center, throw open the doors of the Juilliard School, and show those people how a violin ought to sound.

And now I almost want to laugh. Or cry.

What pride. And what ignorance—to think everything was going to just trot along like the pony ride at the state fair in Lewisburg, to think that Lizzy would get to marry Mr. Darcy in real life. And to think that I could keep telling myself my own perfect little story.

Right. Think again.

I know that I'll go and take that audition at Juilliard tomorrow. I'm not a no-show. I'd still go if both my arms were broken.

But I don't kid myself. I know I'm not ready, mentally or musically. So I'll have to muddle my way through.

My cell phone rings, and blue light fills the room.

All these calls. Everybody means well, I know that. And everyone wants to say how sorry they are about Grampa. But I don't want to talk to one more person about him. I don't want to share those memories. I need to keep that part of my story for myself.

It's on the fourth ring now, and I want to whip the thing against the wall.

But like a nice little girl, I flip open the phone.

"Hello?"

"Hi, is this Gwen? This is Alicia. Bobby gave me your number. Is this a good time?"

"Oh—hi . . . sure, this is good. Robert talks about you all the time." Which feels like the right thing to say to a girlfriend when she's there and he's here.

She giggles. "Robert. I keep forgetting that he's trying to use his *professional* name now." Another giggle, and there's a whiff of sarcasm in her voice. I like her.

She says, "Anyway, *Bobby* said it's been a rough couple of days. And I'm so sorry about your grandfather. But that's not why I called. Bobby said if I asked, maybe you'd play a little violin for me. Over the phone. He said I should request the fast caprice."

I can't help smiling. "He's trying to be my big helper, and he's recruited you to cheer me up, right?"

She laughs, a beautiful sound. "That's my Bobby . . . and your Robert. Not very subtle, but sweet. But I wouldn't have called if I didn't really want to hear you play. Bobby says you're a great violinist, and he never exaggerates, at least not about music. So, how about it?"

"It's going to take me a minute or two to get ready. Want to wait?"

"Minutes, hours, days—I'm all ears." Again, that trace of irony.

I toss the phone on the bed, flip on the light, and run upstairs to get my violin.

My dad's in front of the TV, and he says, "Hey there, you gonna play for me now? How 'bout somethin' by Bach?"

"A little later, Daddy," and I'm back down the stairs.

Talking loud toward the phone, I say, "I'm opening the case . . . and this is a quick pluck or two to check the tuning . . . and now I have to get the bow tight, and it needs a little rosin." I pick up the phone, and say, "Could you hear any of that?"

"Loud and clear. And this is by Paganini, right?"

"Right. He's this wild, romantic Italian guy, a real genius, like a violin rock star. And he wrote these twenty-four solo pieces back around 1800, and they're just incredible. And impossible. So here goes. This is caprice number two."

I bring two pillows to the edge of my bed, put the phone on top of them, stand up straight, set my bow, take a deep breath, and begin.

The fast caprice. And it is, because it's all sixteenth notes, and it dips and sweeps and skips all over the fingerboard. It's been over twenty-four hours since I've played, probably the longest break I've had in years, but

I'm hearing and feeling every note, and every hair on the bow is alive and speaking. And the insane double-stops and the nonstop octaves that constantly challenge the melody—it's all flowing, and the music is pouring out.

It's when I'm riding my bow on this wild climb up the fingerboard, and it's when I'm skidding down the other side—that's when I'm suddenly hearing Charlie Daniels, and he's playing "The Devil Went Down to Georgia," the instrumental section in the middle. Because this caprice and that song, they're blood brothers, with the same sizzle and pop and showmanship, except the bearded guy with the leather hat plays *so* much faster.

And when I'm almost to the end, and I'm out there on the edge of the musical universe, and I start trying to re-enter the atmosphere so I can land this song, there's Charlie again, running side by side with Paganini. And I'm thinking that I'd pay a million dollars if just once I could see old Niccolò up there on the stage of *Austin City Limits*, just him and Charlie Daniels, both of them setting their strings on fire.

And when I finally drop into the wrenching, clenching, double-stopped finish of the caprice, I can't quite believe what I've just heard. And felt. Because it's been three minutes of pure beauty. And I played that piece with my whole self, my whole heart.

And I played it with the lights on.

I pick up the phone. But for ten seconds, maybe fifteen, I can't talk. Because something new just happened, something important.

Alicia doesn't talk either.

Finally I clear my throat and say, "So, that was it."

She's quiet another few moments. "That was . . . it was just beautiful. Really. Thank you. Perfect. And Bobby's right about you. I'm sure of it." Then she pauses. "Bobby told me that you know what happened' to him. Two years ago."

"Yes, and he told you about the man that showed up here? In the city?"

"Yes, he told me. Scary."

Then I say, "Look, I hope this isn't too personal or anything, but when Robert disappeared for all those weeks—like, afterwards, did he change? From the experience?"

She thinks a second or two, and says, "He didn't do a Jekyll and Hyde or anything, if that's what you mean. But yes, there was a change. Like with music? Before it happened, he liked to play the trumpet, and he was in the jazz band at his school and everything. But then afterwards, it just started to mean more to him. He got serious about music. That's what I think changed—he got more serious, about a lot of things. And he thinks more. We both do."

I don't know what to say next, but she can tell, and she saves me.

"Well, listen, thanks again for my private concert. I

loved it. And I hope we can really meet someday. Because I want to hear you play in person. And I want to talk more, okay?"

"Sure," I say, "I'd like that," and I mean it. "And thanks for calling. And thank *Bobby* for putting you up to it."

We both laugh, and then say good-bye.

Gifts. Moments like this are gifts. A person calls from a thousand miles away, and it feels like a friend, and suddenly there's some light again.

I dig around in my shoulder bag so I can check my list of audition times for the millionth time. And in the bag I see the letter, the one from the envelope Grampa sent to Mr. Grant. I stuffed it in there at the end of the meeting at the police station.

My name's on the front, blue ink in Grampa's shaky writing. It's almost too precious to tear open. And I nearly don't, because, really, what else could Grampa possibly say to me? Or give to me?

But I can't resist, and there's a single sheet of paper with something folded inside. At first I think he's giving me one of Grandmother's necklaces. But I unfold the paper, and his army dog tags drop onto the bed, the ones he wore for six years during World War II.

So far tonight, a blind girl who doesn't complain about her life has made me laugh from a thousand miles away; and now my grampa, who never once complained about anything, has made me cry from somewhere else, somewhere beyond a thousand miles away.

But I dry my eyes, and I pick up my borrowed violin and bow, and I walk down to the basement, and I knock on the rehearsal room door.

And when Robert opens it, I smile and say, "Time's up. I've got an audition tomorrow."

chapter 18

GREATER LOVE

On Tuesday morning I wake up early. I don't touch my violin. I don't even look at it. I shower and dress and go upstairs. I'm not hungry, but I force myself to eat two eggs and a piece of toast anyway. There's not much talk.

After breakfast I get my case, and at the door, Robert gives me a hug, and he says, "I know you'll do great. You will."

And then Daddy and I walk over to Broadway and get a cab.

Ten minutes later we're walking across the plaza at Lincoln Center. Alice Tully Hall, the Metropolitan Opera, Avery Fisher Hall. Some of the best musicians in the world will be rehearsing and performing here all week long.

It makes me feel small.

In the lobby of the school, I check in at the tables along the back wall, and then Daddy and I sit down to wait. My accompanist comes and asks if I want to find a practice room and warm up. It's probably a good idea, but I'd rather be still.

I'm glad my dad is here. This is not his world at all, and he's completely unimpressed. And that helps me. No matter what happens here today, cars will still be expertly repaired at the Pro Shop Garage off Interstate 79 near Elkview, West Virginia. No matter what, life will go on. It's good to remember that.

I reach into the pocket of my jacket, then open my palm in Daddy's direction and say, "Look what Grampa gave me."

He takes the dog tags, squints to read them, and then runs his fingers across the stamped lettering.

"It's not a small thing, to give these up. You know that, right?"

I nod, but I hold back my feelings. It's not the right moment to be getting all emotional.

Then Daddy says, "You find the hidden message yet?"

"What? What message?"

He turns the ID over and taps his thick fingernail against the dull metal above Grampa's name. I take it from him and bring it up close. And I see something, scratched into the stainless steel, maybe by a pin or the point of a knife, years and years ago. There are lots of other small scratches, and the surface is worn so smooth that I have to catch the light just right to see anything at all. Out loud, I say, "J . . . 15 . . . 13, right?"

My dad nods.

"What's it mean?"

He shakes his head, then he taps the middle of his chest and I hear a metallic clink. "Scratched the same thing on my own tags the day I got 'em. Secret code. Soldier stuff. But I'll give y'a clue. That J? It *doesn't* stand for Jesus."

My dad doesn't have a subtle bone in his body, which is one of the reasons I love him so much.

I say, "So it's a Bible verse, right?" Another nod. "And the J stands for . . . Joshua?" Nothing. "Judges?" Nothing. "Job? . . . Jeremiah?"

I know my books of the Bible, and I run through the rest of the J's in order. Nothing, until I say, "John?" And there's a flicker of a smile. "So it's John 15, verse 13, right?"

"Can't say. Secret code. Soldier stuff."

"Come on, Daddy. Tell me. Please?"

But he shakes his head. "Oughta know your Bible better."

I look at the clock, and I've got seventeen minutes. So I grab the tags and I say, "Save my seat."

Because I want to know this. Right now. It feels important. Everything feels important right now.

And there's got to be a Bible somewhere close. Because New York City has everything, even Bibles.

I'm out the door, and as I trot past the fountain at the center of the plaza, I think there has to be a bookstore within a block or two. Then I look up, and I adjust my course, because now I know where I'm going: just across

Columbus, straight toward the fifteen-foot-high red neon letters that say Hotel Empire.

In two minutes I'm at the front desk, and in four minutes a friendly woman in a housekeeper's uniform is handing me a Bible, courtesy of the Gideons.

I sit in a huge red chair and open the book. Matthew, Mark, Luke, John, John 12, John 14, John 15.

And there's verse 13. And it's so simple, one sentence. Soldier stuff.

Greater love hath no man than this,
that a man lay down his life for his friends.

Walking back across Columbus Avenue, the tears are streaming down my face. Because now I know.

I know why Grampa tucked himself into that foxhole last Thursday. He did it for me. He knew he was going, and he hid himself so it wouldn't make a commotion. He tried to buy me a few more precious days of harmony and order, peace and quiet. If he could have moved all the mountains of West Virginia and brought them here to shelter me, he would have. But in the end, he hoped that one or two more days in my little practice room would be enough. And it was.

Grampa said the people who loved him and cared for him would understand. And now I do. Because now I have a whole story.

I have my own story, and I love my story, but I know I can't tell it alone, not now. Because stories have centers, but they don't have edges. No boundaries. And I needed to learn that. Thank you, Grampa. And Mama. And Daddy. And Mr. Richards and Pyotr. And Robert, and Alicia too. Even William.

No edges.

Passing the fountain, I slip the chain over my head and tuck Grampa's tags inside my white shirt. A minute later, my eyes wiped dry, I walk back into the lobby of the school. I sit down again next to my dad, and when I take his hand, he turns and smiles at me.

Five minutes later a woman at the registration table calls my name.

I pick up my violin case, and I nod and smile at my accompanist, because she's part of my story too. Together we walk to the elevator, ride to the third floor, then take a right along the corridor to find Room 311.

And I am not afraid. I can play.